Murder Ship

by

G. H. Teed

George Heber Hamilton Teed (1886-1938)

First Published 1935

Stillwoods Edition

Stillwoods.Blogspot.Ca
GHTeed.Blogspot.Com

Catalogue Information:
Title: Murder Ship
Author: G. H. Teed (George Heber Hamilton Teed (1886-1938))
First Published by Stanley Smith Ltd., London, 1935
This Edition: Stillwoods, 2018
ISBN Canada: 978-1-988304-56-4
Author blog: http://ghteed.blogspot.com/
Blog: Stillwoods.Blogspot.Ca
Storefront: http://www.lulu.com/spotlight/lulubook22

Originally Dedicated to Bunny

Sir Charles Gilson has designed and built a floating aerodrome that is to be placed mid-Atlantic so that aircraft can travel between Africa and South America or Europe and North America, in this 1930s thriller. But there are those out to thwart his being the first to do so. Grant Rushton is sent in to ensure his success. But there are so many against them!

This novel was written by the master thriller writer, G. H. Teed. Teed who wrote hundreds of thrillers for Sexton Blake mysteries and Nelson Lee stories so popular at newstands in England from 1915 to 1940.

Somewhere in those magazines this story is to be found.

CHAPTER I

WHEN a regal ship like the new leviathan, *Corsair,* starts on a luxury cruise it is natural to assume that the fortunate passengers may expect a beguiling voyage in which no pains will be spared to administer to their comfort and pleasure.

It can also be anticipated that, before the cruise is finished, there will have been born and died, many little plants that thrive upon the weaknesses of human emotions—romantic attachments, some of them hot and brief, some light and trifling, and some deep and suffering at the withering touch of death.

One does not look, however, for anything of a seriously tragic nature in a vast, floating hotel where every possible amenity is provided, where everything is light and laughter and music, where cares are supposed to be carried away on the first burst of the sea breeze.

On the maiden voyage of the *Corsair,* however, although every possible effort had been made to anticipate the demands of those who had been fortunate enough to secure bookings, and although the ship left Southampton under the best possible auguries, that maiden voyage was to record a series of dreadful and tragic happenings before it was finished.

For not all those who travelled in her were there for simple recreation.

The tall, good looking, well-tailored man who was down in the passenger list as 'Mr. Grant Rushton,' did not come aboard at Southampton with the bulk of the passengers. He slipped up the gangway quietly at Cherbourg where the *Corsair* had put in for a brief call to pick up the complement from France.

His main luggage, however (all but a small blue case which he carried) was in his cabin, and to this he proceeded immediately he set foot on deck.

The 'cabin' was, in fact, a most luxuriously arranged suite of bedroom, sitting-room and bathroom, with a tiny enclosed balcony all its own, and a small vestibule as one entered from the corridor. It was one of the three finest suites in the ship.

The late arrival did not keep the steward waiting long.

"I shall not dine in the restaurant to-night," he said curtly. "By the way, what is your name?"

"Winchell, sir. I have been allotted specially to you, sir."

"Very well, Winchell. Bring me something here, anything that you choose will do; and some whisky and soda—with cracked ice. And please remember, Winchell, that I receive no visitors."

"Very good, sir."

The man vanished with extraordinary quiet, but Grant Rushton stood in the middle of the sitting-room until he heard the outer vestibule door close. Then, still clutching his case, he opened the door, towards which his back had been turned, and stepped into the bedroom.

It was more like the sleeping apartment of a de luxe hotel than a cabin on board ship, but there is little difference in these days between what money will buy ashore and afloat.

One of the twin beds had been removed, making the place really spacious. It was carpeted with a beautiful Turkey rug, furnished in gleaming mahogany with a well fitted desk and chair in one corner. Beyond was the door leading to the bathroom and, on the right, two windows, rather than portholes, one of them a long french window, opening on to that section of the private balcony.

These were, at the moment, obscured by drawn blinds, but the moment Rushton had locked the door behind him, he laid the case on the bed and went to the two windows.

He shot up the blinds and saw that both were locked. But even this did not satisfy him for, unlocking the french window, he stepped out on to the balcony and peered about him.

On his left there was a partition shutting it off from the next section of the deck. On the right it extended past similar windows in the sitting-room to another partition. It seemed beautifully private.

When he was satisfied that the space was quite deserted, he re-entered the sleeping cabin, closed and locked the french window and drew the blinds.

Next he walked to the door leading to the sitting-room and, laying his ear against it, stood listening. He could hear someone moving softly about and knew that Winchell had already returned with the first part of the service.

A brief glance at the door showed him that it was quite impossible for anyone to spy upon him.

There was no keyhole visible on the inner side, the door locking with an automatic catch when it was closed and only capable of being opened from the other side by one possessing the proper key. Such a key had been in the narrow slit of a lock when Rushton entered but it was now in his pocket. Winchell, of course, would also have a key.

His next care was to investigate the bathroom, an inviting place where, Rushton told himself, he would revel presently. But it held nothing to cause him apprehension so, closing that door, he turned back into the sleeping cabin.

He stood for a moment looking at his main luggage that had been neatly piled by the steward. It could remain as it was for the present. He had something more important to attend to.

Walking lightly to the desk, he drew out the chair and sat down. Again, he paused as if listening and, hearing what sounded like the tinkle of glass in the outer cabin, he leant forward a little and took hold of the handle of the lower right hand drawer.

On being drawn almost fully open it was revealed as being perfectly empty, waiting for the tenant's personal material to be put in.

But Rushton did not seem to be interested in its emptiness. In fact, he scarcely glanced into the drawer. Instead, he bent still lower so that he could thrust his hand in a considerable distance and then upwards so that his fingers touched the dustboard separating it from the drawer above.

But his exploring fingers encountered something else. They came into contact with a small piece of folded paper that had been secured to the dustboard by a flat drawing pin. Rushton loosened it and drew out pin and paper.

He thrust the pin quickly into a waistcoat pocket and unfolded the paper—it was no more than three inches square and had been folded only once.

But it was what Rushton had expected to find, what he knew should have been placed there while the ship lay at Southampton, for him to find when he came aboard at Cherbourg.

It contained only a few words, which he scanned closely. Then, while still holding it in his hand, he drew out a pocket lighter, snapped it open and held the paper to the flame.

It flared up so suddenly and became completely consumed so quickly that one would think the paper had been treated with some highly inflammable matter to ensure just such swift destruction—which, indeed, was the case.

Rushton caught the small quantity of ash in the palm of his hand, and, after rubbing it to indecipherable dust with the point of a finger, dropped the residue in the waste-paper basket.

He leant down again and closed the drawer. Then, straightening up, he was about to rise when, in the glass of a large picture of a sailing ship that hung over the desk, he saw reflected the door leading to the sitting-room just beginning to open slowly.

He stiffened. It could not be the steward. He would never enter in that fashion.

He had felt reasonably safe from that direction while Winchell was busy in the next cabin.

Next, he sprang to his feet, the chair going over with a soft thud as he did so. His hand shot in under his coat as if he were reaching for a shoulder holster but, before his fingers could grasp any weapon, a hand came in through the opening, a curious looking, blued steel bit of metal appeared and then there sounded what was extraordinarily like the light cough of a nervous child.

One—two—three.

The sound could not have been heard a dozen yards away and, certainly, not through the walls, windows or doors of the suite.

Then, as Rushton reeled sideways and fell to the floor, the weapon was withdrawn, the door closed, and for a brief moment there was silence.

But now a most extraordinary thing happened. The bullets that had been discharged by the strange and almost completely silent weapon, had struck Grant Rushton full in the back. They had been carried with a velocity and foot-poundage at muzzle that were sufficient to knock a buffalo cold.

And it is certain that the one who had fired the shots must have felt satisfied that the deed had been successfully done from the manner in which the victim had crashed to the carpet.

Nor had there been any sham about that fall. The speed and weight of the bullets had sent him down as if he had been pole-axed, but that was all. Not one had penetrated the very fine, light but marvellously effective bullet-proof chain shirt he was wearing.

The door had scarcely closed when Rushton rolled over and got groggily to his feet. He caught hold of the desk with one hand as if to steady himself, while, with the other, he drew from an armpit holster an automatic pistol.

With every sign of the effort requiring all his reserves of strength and will power, he reeled to the door of the sitting-room and turned the spring catch.

Then, with his weapon upraised, he lurched into the outer cabin. It was empty. The table was partially laid for a meal, but the steward was not to be seen.

Rushton continued to the small entrance vestibule and opened the door leading into the corridor.

Flinging open the door he was about to plunge into the corridor when, immediately in his path, a little old lady threw her hands in the air and, with a terrified look at his gun, began to emit hysterical screams.

There is no doubt that Rushton must have presented a somewhat terrifying sight as he appeared in such sudden fashion, brandishing a gun and now, instead of looking for his would-be murderer, he found all his time and persuasion employed in soothing the frightened woman.

In a flash he thrust the gun out of sight, then he broke into apologies, assuring her earnestly that she had nothing to fear and making up the first excuse that came into his mind.

While he was engaged in this, for him, strange and awkward task, his steward appeared, accompanied by the stewardess. It was now that Rushton discovered that the frightened lady was his immediate neighbour, her suite being the one directly across from his.

He was only too pleased to resign his responsibility to the stewardess, and viewed with relief the old lady's disappearance behind her own door.

Nevertheless, those few moments during which he had lain half stunned on the floor, and this delay through the old lady's hysterics, had been more than sufficient for his would-be murderer to escape in some direction or other.

CHAPTER II

BACK in his own cabin he stood watching the steward while he set down the tray and rearranged the few things.

He had no doubt that Winchell was curious as to what had taken him into the corridor and why his neighbour had been in such an upset state. But Rushton decided not to enlighten him. Let the stewardess tell him whatever explanation the old lady might give.

But the fact that someone could enter the suite so easily was another matter.

"How long were you out of the suite?" he asked abruptly.

Winchell looked up in surprise.

"Only a few minutes, sir."

"Why did you leave the door unlocked?"

"But I didn't leave it unlocked, sir. I locked it and took the key away in my pocket."

"All right, perhaps I was mistaken."

When the steward had gone, Rushton bolted the vestibule door and made for the inner cabin. He went straight to the pile of luggage which, until now, he had not examined.

Placing them side by side, he took out his bunch of private keys and opened them. Then, with quick fingers, he turned over the contents of each, noting keenly as he did so, just how each item was placed. For he knew exactly how each had been packed.

He didn't have to finish the job to know that between Southampton and Cherbourg, during the brief period in which he had been separated from them, someone had gone through them very thoroughly and with an eye to replacing the various articles so as to make them appear undisturbed.

But Rushton had arranged the packing expecting just such a contingency, and there were many ways, impossible for anyone else to know, in which he could detect positively that they had been interfered with.

He slammed the lid of the trunk and, rising, lit a cigarette. He didn't bother investigating the blue morocco case that he had brought on board with him. That hadn't been out of his possession one instant.

But the attack upon him and the fact that, thus early in the cruise, his luggage had been searched, was all the proof he needed to tell him that he was already marked down.

Although he wasn't quite sure of the steward, be did not believe the fellow was in the pay of those who had attacked him. He had been picked specially for this job by the commander of the ship who had vouched for him as being thoroughly reliable and discreet. Nevertheless, the fact remained, that not only had someone found it possible to enter his suite and spend considerable time going through his luggage, but also to choose the few moments when the steward was absent to slip in and plug him three times.

It argued a close knowledge of the suite and his movements, and that was the sort of thing Grant Rushton didn't fancy, particularly when engaged on the kind of business that occupied him just now.

Sitting down at the desk, he took from a waistcoat pocket a small folder of what looked exactly like cigarette papers. Indeed, had one glanced at the red cover one would have seen the name of a well-known brand of such papers.

Rushton carefully abstracted one of the flimsy sheets and, taking a pencil from another pocket, he wrote four words: 'MUST SEE YOU TO-NIGHT.'

Then, folding the paper, he took the drawing pin and stuck the message to the dustboard above the bottom drawer of the desk where he had found the other paper on entering.

In the outer cabin he hurriedly ate a few scraps of food, helped himself to drink, and slipped into a loose travelling coat and soft hat.

Switching out all the lights and locking all the doors he made his way along the side corridor to the main gangway, and from there to the lift that would take him to the main promenade deck.

On his way, he passed the entrance to the restaurant. It was brilliantly lighted, with most of the tables full. On his left was the ball-room where several couples were dancing to a lively fox-trot.

Through all was the lilt and laughter of carefree voices, and it would seem difficult to believe that, only a few minutes before, there had been a very definite attempt at murder on board.

Rushton stepped out on to the deck. His first glance was over the rail where the water was a black torment, broken by curving white patches where the great ship ploughed through it.

But, over it, was a mist that Rushton knew would thicken to fog before long. Indeed, as he made his way down the deck towards the smoke-room, wisps of vapour were already showing against the lights.

He stepped into the smoke-room which, at the dinner hour, did not contain more than a dozen or so late diners and bridge fiends.

Rushton approached the cocktail bar, and ordered a sidecar, then, while he sipped the drink, he gave the place the once-over. No face was familiar to him. The majority seemed to be just the type one would expect to see upon a rather lengthy cruise such as the *Corsair* was bound upon, a little more sophisticated and, probably, in somewhat better circumstances than those one would have found upon a shorter cruise.

But that did not eliminate any one from Rushton's calculations. He knew that the person or persons who were so eager for his death might appear in any guise, that even now, he might be in the presence of the one who had plugged him already.

He ordered a second cocktail and lit a cigarette. One or two other persons came in from the deck and appeared to be casting about for a game of bridge.

Three or four who had been drinking cocktails went off to dinner and, shortly after he finished his second cocktail, Rushton made for the door.

The instant he stepped out on to the deck he saw that his anticipations about the fog had already been realised. A thick blanket had descended upon the ship, one of those sudden curtains that the Channel can drop with little warning. And, just as the door slammed behind him, Rushton heard the dismal dirge of the siren.

He intended to take a more detailed look in the restaurant and the ball-room before he went below so, turning up his collar against the driving damp, he started forward.

He bumped into someone before he had gone half a dozen steps. There were mutual apologies and he passed on without being able to distinguish more than the voice of the other.

Another dozen strides or so and, without the slightest warning, someone sprang upon him from behind.

Rushton was a powerful and active man who had handled many a surprise attack in his time. But this leap had come so silently and so unexpectedly that he had no more than time to stiffen against it when he felt something driven against his shoulder blades with terrific force.

A strong wrist had driven that stab but, for the second time that night, Rushton's mail shirt saved him. Before his assailant could stab again Rushton had twisted round.

Luck was with him for, as he shot out his hand he felt his fingers close about the wrist that held the knife. His right hand grasped the smooth, but hard, material of a coat and then, foiled in his first purpose, the other strained furiously and savagely to squirm from Rushton's hold.

But Rushton held on, driving his man back and back, step by step until he had him almost at the rail, his object being to cramp him against that, and then free his right hand for punching.

But the other seemed to guess his purpose. For a moment or two he seemed to give way more quickly then, as Rushton made to slam him against the side, he brought up one knee into Rushton's groin with a force that turned him suddenly sick and weak.

Rushton made a savage grasp with his hand, striving to hang on until he could recover from the effects of the foul blow. But his assailant dragged free with such furious determination that one button was torn from his coat and left in Rushton's grasp.

Rushton felt another savage blow from the knife, then the fellow vanished as swiftly as he had come, put to flight, Rushton guessed, by the sound of laughing voices as other passengers came along the deck.

CHAPTER III

RUSHTON did not pause as he had intended to have a look at the passengers in the restaurant and ball-room.

He made his way to the lift, trying not to limp in yielding to the throbbing pain in his groin.

Stepping out at his own deck he went along and let himself into his suite. He bolted the vestibule door and switched on the lights.

Everything seemed just as he had left it. He unlocked the other door and stepped into the sleeping cabin. Closing the door so that the lock snapped into place he went to the desk and, thrusting his fingers into the lower drawer, found a piece of paper pinned to the top partition. He did not know if it was the one he had left until he had unfolded it. Then he knew that it was an answer to the one he had affixed before leaving the suite.

He frowned in puzzlement as he read the few words that were written, for they said:

"ENTER YOUR BATHROOM. TAP ON THE LONG MIRROR AT THE END."

Rushton touched the flame of his pocket lighter to it as before and, when it was consumed, rubbed the ashes before allowing them to fall into the waste-paper basket.

Slipping out of his coat and tossing his hat on to the bed, he stepped into the bathroom, closed the door and bolted it after him, then walked past the tub until he was close to a pier glass that had been set in the wall at the end, occupying, indeed, almost the whole width of the narrow space.

Tap, tap-tap, tap, tap-tap, tap, tap-tap.

Thrice he gave the one, one-two signal, then waited. He was not left long. Within a few moments there reached him a slight sound on the other side of the mirror and then the whole glass swung away from him to reveal an exactly similar bathroom on the other side.

Facing him was a small, elderly man with white moustache and white pointed beard. But if his body was frail, his eyes revealed the courage of a lion. It was Sir Charles Gilson, owner of the Gilson Line of which the *Corsair* was now the pride.

He moved back so that Rushton could step through the opening. Sir Charles closed the panel and jerked his hand towards the other door.

10

"Green and Follet are having a bite to eat in the outer cabin. You and I can talk in the sleeping cabin. I thought it wiser not to tell even you about this secret panel. No one else knows but Captain Forbes. What has happened?"

Rushton did not answer until they were in the other cabin, a sleeping apartment very much like his own though somewhat larger. Then, turning round, he indicated the back of his coat.

"I've been on board about an hour," he said laconically. "Those holes are where I was plugged three times and I fancy you will be able to see the slit from a dagger stab."

Sir Charles gave a low whistle.

"They haven't lost much time, have they?"

"Not much. But that isn't all. Somewhere, between Southampton and Cherbourg, my luggage was searched thoroughly."

"Well, they didn't find much there."

"No, sir. But it shows that my movements are known intimately. There has been a bad leak somewhere. What worries me is the possibility of that same knowledge extending to your presence on board."

They were facing each other now.

"How could they know that?" asked Sir Charles. "It was given out publicly that I had gone up to Scotland for a month. I was smuggled aboard secretly in the middle of the night at Southampton. That was before any passengers were permitted on the dock. Not a soul on board knows but Captain Forbes, the chief steward and the steward who is looking after this suite, and I can trust them to the limit. Do you think you were trailed from London to Paris or from Paris to Cherbourg?"

"I tell you, sir, it was known before the ship left Cherbourg that I would be on board. How else would they know about my luggage? And, another thing. Unless Winchell is a traitor, then my movements—and his—were closely watched from the moment I came up the gangway at Cherbourg. The first attack made upon me was within a quarter of an hour of my entering the suite and during a matter of five minutes or so that Winchell was absent. I don't want to worry you about these things. I shall handle my end of it. But I thought it best to warn you without delay so that you could know what had happened. I still feel, sir, that there has been a leakage of information of things that are vital to you."

"I can't imagine how that could be. Not even Frick, my confidential assistant, knew about the plans. I have always kept that to myself and, anyway, he is thoroughly trustworthy. Nor would anyone else in the office betray anything even if they knew it, which they don't."

"Well, sir, there is a very determined enemy on board. What is the latest of the floating aerodrome?"

"I had a wireless this evening. The tugs with the drome in tow left Las Palmas to-day. It is a slow job and they ought to be just about at the anchoring spot in the South Atlantic by the time we get there. It is your job, Rushton, to deal with any enemies who may be on board. Green and Follet are working on the plans steadily. They know what is required and will be able to complete the work by the time we get to the anchoring spot."

"What about the appliances, sir? Do you think there is any chance of the enemy getting at them?"

"Not a chance. The cases are stored in the strong room. No one can approach them. And, when Green and Follet and I are not working on the plans they are in my personal possession. With Green and Follet sleeping in the outer cabin, myself in here with the plans under my pillow with a gun, and you in the other suite flanking this, I don't see how they can do anything."

"What they attempted to-night, sir, proves that they are ready to go to any lengths. But I shall lose no time in trying to identify them. If anything comes up I'll communicate in the usual way."

"Come and speak to Green and Follet before you go."

Rushton followed Sir Charles into the outer cabin where, at the central table, two men sat in their shirt sleeves. Both wore glasses and were strongly of a similar stamp (though they were not even distantly related)—thin, sandy, clean shaven, of medium height one would say, studying them as they sat.

One end of the large table was laid with some food. The other was bare and, on this, were some blue-prints about twelve inches square. There were also some drawing instruments such as are employed by mechanical draughtsmen.

Rushton had met both before. He knew them as Sir Charles's confidential experts who were employed now in studying those plans which, until he boarded the *Corsair*, Sir Charles had kept secret even from his most trusted associate. Not even Rushton, whose job it was to protect Sir Charles and them, had ever seen them before.

The shipowner told the two engineers briefly of what had happened to Rushton.

"It proves that I did not warn you too strongly," he added. "Those people who are after these things will stop at nothing. I'd like to let you fellows out for a breath of air, but this is enough to warn me that you'd better remain in here. You'll have to get what air you can on the balcony outside."

They nodded together. It didn't seem to bother them that they must remain shut up in the suite. Their interest seemed to be concentrated entirely on the plans before them. And well might that be, for they represented something that engineers all over the world had been striving to find—and Sir Charles had reached the goal first.

Those bits of blue-prints represented what might be the control of the air traffic between Europe and America. There was no secret that rich and influential interests on the Continent, in North and South America and in England (as represented by Sir Charles Gilson) had been running a hectic race to be first with a floating aerodrome that could be anchored in mid-Atlantic and retained there without fear of the worst gales that might blow.

It was known, too, that Sir Charles had devised and built a massive floating drome that was even now being towed out to the anchorage spot in the South Atlantic, the one about which he had told Rushton he had been advised that day.

But it was also known that the drome afloat was no more than a useless shell until certain vital parts were fitted, parts that would serve to stabilise it so as to ride immune from any gale and, further, a secret system of internal action that would keep the surrounding sea calm in any weather.

The secret of those vital parts was on those blueprints. Sir Charles was right when he said that not a soul had seen them or even guessed at their secret until he had placed them before Green and Follet that same day.

With his own hands, he had planned the necessary castings and, bit by bit, had had them made until he had collected the lot. And now those parts, waiting for the moment when the *Corsair* should pause in the South Atlantic, were in the strong room of the ship.

With a certain subsidy of a hundred thousand pounds annually for landing service to international aeroplanes and the prospect of either the control of the ocean air mail throughout the world or enormous royalties from various governments, it is little wonder that there were desperate people out to get possession of those few bits of paper that held the secret.

Back in his own cabin, Rushton lit a cigarette and set his thoughts to the puzzle that had been nagging him ever since the first attack.

On analysis, he came back each time to the fact that it would have been too much of a stroke of luck for his would-be murderer to choose by chance the exact moment when Winchell would be out of the cabin for a few minutes.

It looked strongly as though someone had been on watch and had known what moment to choose.

But how? Not from any point in the passage. Then, from some other cabin?

That was a thing that must be settled.

And here was another puzzle.

He took from his pocket the button that he had torn from the coat of the person who had attacked him in the fog.

It was an ordinary black bone button such as one would find on a blue suit or black jacket.

There was one thing about it, however, that caught Rushton's eye particularly. His impression was that most buttons in ordinary use possessed four holes for the thread, whereas, in this case, there were only two.

He glanced down at the buttons on his own coat. Each, he saw, was perforated with four holes, as he had thought. Then it came to him that this sort of button he held in his fingers was more a type used on the Continent than in England, but he could not be sure on that point.

Attached to it, were some shreds of cloth that had come away in the violent tug, not many, but enough for him to be able to identify the sort of cloth used in the coat. It was black in shade and, he thought, from a weave that was either serge or hopsack.

He was still examining button and cloth when, suddenly, his gaze was attracted by something white that was moving at the bottom of the vestibule door.

In an instant he was on his feet, speeding towards the spot. He soon saw that it was a small, square envelope that someone had just pushed under the door.

Swiftly he thrust back the bolts and peered out into the passage. Not a soul was in sight.

He raced along to where the short passage debouched into the main gangway but, beyond a steward in the distance, he saw no one.

Rushton returned to his suite and made to close the door. He was both angry and baffled. For the second or third time someone had found it possible to approach close to him without his being able to do a thing to hinder the unknown.

He bent to pick up the envelope that he had left lying on the floor but, to his amazement, could not locate it.

With a muttered imprecation, he pushed the door wide open and looked all about. Then he stepped into the passage to search there, thinking it possible that, in his haste, he had inadvertently kicked it over the sill.

But, nowhere, inside or out, could he find the thing and, more angry than ever, he was about to close the door of the vestibule when his gaze happened to fall on the handle of the opposite door. He stood rigid, watching it intently.

It was perfectly still now but he could have sworn that, a moment before, he had seen the handle moving, just as if someone on the other side had released their fingers very cautiously.

CHAPTER IV

RUSHTON was more perturbed than he cared to admit over the mysterious appearance of that envelope and its still more puzzling disappearance.

Who had pushed it under the door? And who had snapped it up during the few moments when he was out in the main corridor?

They were two simple, elementary questions but, just now, a great deal seemed to hinge on their answers.

As far as he knew, the only person who could possibly have carried out such an operation under the conditions existing, would have to come from the suite opposite his own, the only other one down that branch corridor.

But the tenant of that was the little old lady whom he had frightened so a little earlier. Surely she could not be suspected of such a daring act? Yet—that handle that he thought he had seen move!

Then he thought of the stewardess. Was she still in the other suite? Or what other occupants might there be? That was a question that he must settle without delay.

He rang for Winchell, the steward. When the man appeared, he motioned him to come close.

"Have you seen the stewardess who was looking after my neighbour?"

"Yes, sir. The lady is all right now."

"Did she say why she was frightened?"

"She told stewardess that you appeared very suddenly, sir."

"Nothing else?"

"No, sir, except that she has never travelled alone before and is a little nervous."

"Does she occupy that suite alone then?"

"Yes, sir."

"What do you know about her, Winchell?"

"Only what stewardess has told me, sir. She seems to be a talkative old lady and has told the stewardess all about her affairs and reasons for coming on a cruise."

"What are they, Winchell?"

The steward permitted himself a brief smile. "She says, sir, that she has been tied down to a large family for many years but now, with the last one married, she feels herself entitled to a holiday on her own."

16

"Quite natural. Do you know her name?"

"Mrs. Rentley, sir."

"Very well, Winchell. I shall not want you again to-night."

"Very good, sir."

When the steward was gone again, Rushton lit a cigarette and stood by the table frowning.

There must be an answer to the puzzle, but what was it?

It was obvious that certain persons believed him to be in possession of documents which they were determined to possess. They were prepared to kill him to gain their ends. Two definite attempts had been made to do so during the brief time he had been on board.

But whence had the attacks come?

Further, who had pushed that envelope under the door—and why? And, more than that, who had snatched it during those few moments he had been no more than a dozen yards away?

Rushton's eyes fell on the windows that opened on to the private balcony. He had already tested the fastenings of both the windows and outside shutters but, now, he went to them again.

He immediately made a startling discovery.

The long, french window was now unfastened. Yet he could have sworn positively that it had been locked when he made his examination an hour or so earlier.

Not only that, but the shutters were unfastened as well. He opened the window and, pushing the shutters apart, stepped out on to the balcony.

It was empty enough, from partition to partition. He moved to the rail, peering to right and left and then up and down. It would be possible, he knew, for an acrobatic person to reach any of these private balconies by squirming round one of the partitions or even by dropping down from the deck above or shinning up one of the stanchions from the deck below. It was a thing he could perform himself.

Had someone done that? Had such a person been on the balcony while he was examining the button, and the envelope was being pushed under the door? Had they seen that?

He moved swiftly to the shutters and closed them. Standing close to the slats, he found that he could move them easily so as to get a clear view of the cabin inside. Certainly, it would be possible for anyone standing there to see an envelope being pushed under the vestibule door.

Was that what had happened? Had this unknown person nipped into the cabin to snatch up the envelope and make good his escape during those few vital moments?

If so whom could it be? That unknown could scarcely have been in league with the other unknown who had deposited the envelope.

And, a thing that caused Rushton to frown afresh, was this—who had unfastened the french window and shutters? How had such a person managed it, for it must have been done on the inside? Was it during the time when the shooting attempt had been made while the steward was absent?

Whoever they were, they knew his identity and his purpose for being on board. The fact that they had come into action so soon and were following the thing up with such persistency was proof enough of the determination to 'get' him.

That didn't worry Rushton so much as the danger to Sir Charles Gilson. Was it known that he was on board? If so, then the danger was much more acute. On the other hand, if it was known then why should he be the target for so many attacks?

But what puzzled Rushton more than anything else was the identity of the person who had pushed that envelope under his door. He was savage with himself for not having picked it up before diving into the passage.

Yet, figure how he might, one thing seemed certain. The hand that had struck at him with such deadly purpose and the eye that, he now suspected, had watched him through the shutters, must belong to someone who had means of taking cover very close to his suite.

The suspicion led again and again to the suite across the corridor, but how could one connect such things with the twittering old lady who occupied it?

What had she thought when he appeared so suddenly, brandishing a gun? Winchell had mentioned nothing about that. Was it possible that Mrs. Rentley had not spoken about the gun to the stewardess? If not, why not? Was it just to save him embarrassment? And what would she think was his reason for appearing in such fashion?

Rushton knew that he had to watch everyone and suspect everyone. He wouldn't have been alive now had he not watched his step in the past.

He poured himself a whisky and soda and smoked a final cigarette. By the time, he was ready to turn in he was no nearer a solution than ever.

He made sure enough this time that the windows were fastened and the vestibule door locked and bolted. He also fastened the door connecting the two cabins and, when he tumbled into bed, his gun was within quick reach.

Despite the strenuous evening he had had, and the peril that, he knew, surrounded him, Rushton went off to sleep almost at once.

But, subconsciously, he was alert for the slightest sign of danger. Therefore, when the small buzzer went just over his head, he was awake in an instant.

He pressed the button that controlled the light on the bedside table. His watch showed that it was just a few minutes after midnight.

The buzzer could only be rung from two places, one in the outer cabin and the other in the passage outside the vestibule door.

Alert to any trap, Rushton grabbed his gun and made for the door leading to the outer cabin. Very cautiously, he opened this, reaching for the light switch as he did so. The place proved to be quite empty.

He stepped into the outer cabin, just as the buzzer sounded again—once, twice, thrice, quickly, insistently.

Someone was pressing the button in the passage.

Rushton sped to the vestibule and pushed back the bolts. But, before opening the door, he spoke in a low tone.

"What is it? Who is there?"

No one answered but, instead, there came to his ears the same sound he had heard once before that night, a sound that was like a short, sharp cough. On the previous occasion, it had been caused by the explosion of a silenced gun. What was it now?

He spoke again. Something seemed to bump against the door but no voice answered him.

Turning the key he laid his fingers on the handle and turned. He thrust his gun forward so that he could meet any menace from outside.

Then he eased the door open, and, as he did so, he felt it press against his hand as if some weight were against it. A little more and he saw the reason.

A body lay huddled so close that the head and shoulders came in over the threshold as the support of the door was withdrawn.

Rushton jerked the door wider and pushed into the passage. It was empty. With a wary eye against ambush he made for the main passage. No one to be seen.

Returning to his own door he kept his eye on the door of the suite opposite. It yielded no suggestion at all. Then he gave his attention to the huddled form at his feet.

His first glance showed him the body of a man, dressed, apparently, in a brown monkish robe. A wide-brimmed, low-crowned black felt hat lay a foot or so away where it had fallen. The man's face was hidden for the moment.

Rushton dragged the body into the cabin and closed the door. He was experienced enough in such things to ascertain very quickly that the man was dead, shot through the heart, and that within a very few minutes. He remembered the coughing sound he had heard. Had this crime been committed with the same gun that had been fired at him a little earlier?

He got the body on to the couch and then he got a second shock. For he knew the features.

The man before him had been one of the smoothest criminals on the Continent, a man of great daring and resource who had gone by the name of 'The Brown Priest.'

What was he doing dead outside his door?

Rushton knew that he must send for the doctor quickly. But no doctor could put life back into that corpse. So, with quick practised fingers, he lifted the brown robe and began to make a search of his clothing.

He came upon two curious things almost at once. The first was the discovery that, beneath the brown robe, the man had been wearing a black jacket with black trousers and that the top button of the jacket had been torn away at some time with great violence, so violently, in fact, that a portion of the cloth had come away with it. The remaining buttons were of plain black bone containing only two thread holes instead of four. Rushton took the loose button from his pocket and compared it with the others. It matched perfectly.

His second discovery was an envelope in one pocket of the jacket. It bore no writing but, on a piece of folded paper inside, he saw some words printed in French. They said: 'I will see you at midnight, G.R.'

His own initials and the man had been outside his door at as nearly midnight as might be.

Who had lured him there with that fake message?

CHAPTER V

WHEN he finished his own examination of the Brown Priest, Rushton rang for the steward. When the man came he despatched him for the ship's doctor. He also sent a note to the second in command, Commander Braund, for, the sooner the ship's officers took control of this phase of the matter, the better pleased he would be.

His association with Sir Charles Gilson was secretly known to the commander and to Captain Forbes. Nevertheless, he told the commander as little as was necessary. He wanted to see Sir Charles before he committed himself too far.

It was past two in the morning when, very quietly, the body was removed. It was an incident that must be kept from the passengers in general. Things like that did no good to a luxury ship like the *Corsair.*

But further sleep was out of the question for Rushton. He had plenty to occupy his mind.

Nevertheless, at an early hour the following morning, he was bathed, shaved and ready to go on deck. The fog had lifted and, soon after dawn, Rushton had made a thorough examination of the private balcony outside the suite. Not a trace was there to be seen of any mysterious prowler.

That done, he stood just inside the vestibule door listening to the occasional sounds that reached him from across the corridor. He heard the stewardess come and go several times. Then he heard another knock and a strange voice, a low, husky voice that sounded very attractive.

Still he did not move. But, when he heard definite sounds that told him someone was coming out of the cabin and recognised the voice of the old lady whom he had so startled the evening before, he opened his own door somewhat abruptly and stepped out.

Two women were just leaving the other suite. One was Mrs. Rentley, enveloped in a huge travelling coat and furs, with a veil over her hat that only allowed two rosy cheeks and a pair of bright blue eyes to be seen.

The other was a girl, rather pale, Rushton thought, as if she had been going through the qualms of *mal de mer.* Yet, even in that quick first glance he saw that she was lovely; and that was a lot of thought for Grant Rushton to give to one of the other sex along those lines, for he was no gallant.

He smiled in response to the old lady's greeting.

"It seems we are fated to meet here," she chirruped. "But you are not so terrifying this time."

"I owe you my most profound apologies for startling you so," he assured her. "I hope you are none the worse for it."

"Not at all, not at all, young man. But don't do it again. What is your name?"

"Rushton, madam—Grant Rushton."

"Well, Mr. Rushton, as we are to be neighbours we had better become acquainted. I am Mrs. Rentley and this is my companion, Cara Hume."

Rushton bowed and found the girl's brown eyes fixed on him gravely. He was wondering if her employer had told her about the incident of the night before.

They moved along the passage together but, just as they reached the end where it joined the main gangway, the stewardess came bustling round the bend and, in trying to avoid her, the girl dropped a rug and book she was carrying.

Rushton bent quickly to retrieve the fallen objects. As he picked up the book, he noticed that it had fallen with the cover open and the fly leaf visible, showing the bookmark of the ship's library.

He only had a moment's glance at the leaf but it was enough to show him that it was almost covered with pencilled characters that looked more like hieroglyphics than anything else. Then, as he straightened up, the book was snatched from his hand with a violence that caused him to turn surprised eyes upon the one who did it.

He saw an amazing change in the old lady. She who had been so genial a moment or two before, was now displaying a countenance twisted with sudden passion. Her eyes were blazing upon the girl and she burst out into a tirade that seemed to surprise the girl as much as it did Rushton.

"Stupid, clumsy girl! Why aren't you more careful?"

"But—but, Mrs. Rentley, I didn't know the stewardess was coming."

"No, ma'am, it was quite my fault," broke in the surprised woman. "I'm very sorry. I hope no harm has been done."

The old lady's return to geniality was as amazingly swift as her anger.

"Tut, tut, say no more. I am quick tempered. Don't worry my dear," she added patting the girl's arm. "Perhaps I didn't want this gentleman to see what sort of books a silly old woman enjoys."

She smiled at Rushton who smiled back, for he had been feeling distinctly uncomfortable. Yet he knew that it might all be due to what she had said—quick temper. Heaven knew she had gone into hysterics quickly enough the night before.

Nevertheless, he had been mildly surprised to read the title of the book. *Murders in the Park.* It was, he knew, a good 'thriller' yarn, but not quite the sort of thing he would have expected to find favour with old ladies. Still, in these days, one never knew.

But what did cause Rushton to ponder was, firstly, the fact that someone should have so mutilated the book already and, secondly, the extent of Mrs. Rentley's anger at what was, after all, only a very minor accident.

It was impossible that the book could have been taken out of the library more than very few times at most, for the ship was new and had only been at sea a day or two and there hadn't been time for more than one or two persons to have read it.

Moreover, like every other book in the ship's library, it was a brand new copy. There was nothing about the *Corsair* that wasn't spick and span.

Then what book vandal had filled that fly leaf with pencilled scribblings? Could it have been Mrs. Rentley? Might the fact that she knew Rushton must have seen them account for her anger? And why? Was it because she didn't want him to see how she had mutilated the book? Or was it what she had said—that she didn't want him to learn her taste for such thrilling literature?

The incident passed as swiftly as it had come. On the way up he learned that the girl had been indisposed since coming on board but was all right now, that Mrs. Rentley was making the first sea journey she had ever undertaken and that she had brought along a companion.

He left them in the library, where the only other person besides the library steward, seemed to be a dark, very sleek and prosperous-looking man whom Rushton placed as a South American.

In the smoke-room, Rushton found several men gathered round the bulletin board on which had been pinned the latest wireless news sheets.

At the moment, one of them who looked like a business man from the North, was commenting on one particular item that read:

"It is reported from Bordeaux that the notorious ship known as the 'Ship of the Accursed' has left that port for an unknown destination. None of the criminals on board were allowed to land at Bordeaux though permission was given for stores and fuel to be loaded. It is rumoured that the ship will make for some deserted part of the African or South American coast in order to put ashore secretly the human cargo it carries. It will be recalled that the notorious hell-ship has been turned away from almost every port in Europe."

"What does that mean, anyway?" Rushton heard the man asking.

"That's the ship there's been so much about in the papers," volunteered one. "After that last revolution in the Argentine, the authorities collected all the criminal scum they could find in Buenos Aires and shipped them away, some six hundred I understand. They belong to all nationalities and the ship has been trying to dump them where they came from. But nothing doing —the nations won't own them. So they've been pushing about the sea for six months or more. What is it they call it, oh yes, it says here—the 'Ship of the Accursed.' And, judging from what one reads, they're about the worst bunch of criminals that could be collected together. I'll bet that gang is ripe and ready for anything now."

"That's right," put in another. "They say there isn't one of them that has done less than one murder. It must be a sweet job to keep them under control—like a ship full of wild beasts. If they should break loose—"

"This bulletin says she sailed from Bordeaux yesterday," remarked the first speaker. "If she takes a course straight out into the Atlantic she ought to run pretty close to the course we are following. I hope they won't take it into their heads to tackle us."

Rushton moved on, but he had taken only a few steps when, through the porthole, or, rather, window, he saw two persons that caused him to swing round and dive through the nearest door.

He watched the pair as they went along the deck at a brisk pace and then vanished round the promenade forward. He cut round the end of the smoke saloon so as to reach the other side and there, as he hoped, he saw them coming towards him.

They were a striking couple, the woman particularly. She was tall and lissome and beautifully dressed. A crush hat was pulled down rakishly over hair of that purplish black shade peculiar to some types of southern women. Her eyes were black, her colour rich and warm and she moved with a voluptuous hip movement when walking that

25

completed a picture that was alluring to the last degree.

The man was short and stout, wearing a long, luxuriant beard so common among Frenchmen. It was plentifully sprinkled with grey, as was what one could see of his hair, but his head was covered mostly by a travelling cap that was so huge as to be almost ridiculous. Alone, he would have been almost nondescript. But, with the woman, he fitted as just the right sort of foil.

Rushton knew them well by sight, as they knew him. He knew they passed as the Count and Countess de Saladier, a couple who were seen everywhere on the Continent where Society gathered, who followed the migration from Paris after the Grand Prix to Vichy, then down to Monte Carlo or Cannes and thence to Deauville for August, always mixing with the smartest of the smart set but never quite a part of it.

Rushton had heard many whispers about them. It was said that they lived by their wits, that a good many shady affairs could be traced to them and that the woman was an irresistible bait to draw victims into the trap.

Once he had heard the name connected with a serious and particularly unsavoury affair that developed into one of the worst financial scandals that had ever rocked France. But, if there was any truth in that, the matter had been effectually hushed up.

They would, of course, recognise him. Would they speak? He watched them while they drew nearer and then, suddenly, the woman turned her eyes upon him with a smile that explained in its dazzling fascination why she had been called the 'Orchid.'

"Good morning, monsieur," she said in a rich, contralto voice, and in quite good English.

Rushton lifted his cap and smiled.

"We seem to meet in many places," went on the woman, "but it is the surprise to see Monsieur Rushton on board this ship."

"And to see you," countered Rushton, still smiling.

"We come for the complete change," put in the count, speaking for the first time.

"You will get that in an English ship," observed Rushton.

"It is the fresh experience," agreed the woman.

They were still talking polite nothings when they were interrupted by a page from the wireless office. The count took the message but did not open it. He thrust it into his pocket and bowed to

Rushton. Rushton returned the bow and then, for a moment, his gaze held that of the woman. There was something enigmatic in her smile. Was it mockery, he asked himself?

Rushton continued his way along the deck, racking his brains. There was something he was searching for among the items of the past that lay filed in his memory. Where was it? It came to him in a flash. The Brown Priest! He had seen the Brown Priest with the Saladiers at Monte Carlo some months before. The Brown Priest and the Saladiers—what were they doing on board this English luxury cruiser? There wasn't scope for any profitable bilking at cards among a company such as the *Corsair* carried. It was bigger game than that, that had brought them. Was he the game they were after?

Rushton believed he had struck the real trail at last. He didn't know yet why the Brown Priest had been killed. There might be several reasons to account for that. Perhaps he was on the verge of some treachery. But the secret of the floating drome was just the sort of thing that the Saladiers would go for. They could sell that secret in a ready market for a very large sum of money.

An exhilaration seized Rushton as he felt himself at grips at last with something definite. He almost forgot that he had intended taking out a book from the library until he found himself passing the entrance to the saloon.

He turned in and approached the library steward, stating his requirements.

"A lady left a book here this morning that I'd like to read," he said. "It was called *Murders in the Park*. Will you give it to me, please."

"Sorry, sir, but that is impossible. That book was taken out again almost as soon as it was returned."

"Ah, it seems a popular choice. Do you recall who took it?"

"Yes, sir. It was selected by a gentleman who was sitting here when you and Mrs. Rentley came in. He is a foreigner and wanted anything to read just to practise in English, he said. The book was lying on the table here and he took it."

"It doesn't matter, but the choice was an odd one for a foreigner. I'll take anything."

Rushton chose almost the first volume that came to hand. He stood by the table while the steward wrote his name in the record book and thus was able to read the names of those who had preceded him.

There weren't many this early in the day, only six or seven and, just under Mrs. Rentley's name, he saw that of the passenger who had chosen the book she had returned. 'Mr. Ricardo,' was the name he read.

CHAPTER VI

BACK again in his own suite, Rushton made for the bathroom, locking the doors after him as he went.

In response to his cautious tapping, Sir Charles appeared at the panel connecting the two suites.

Rushton stepped through and followed him into the bedroom.

"I think I've got them," he announced in a whisper.

"What have you found?"

Rushton told him about the Saladiers.

"I'm going to act, at any rate," he added. "But I want to get a closer line on them if possible. While I was talking to them on deck, a wireless message was handed to them. I want to know what is in it. Can you arrange, sir, for me to have copies of all wireless messages that have been received since the ship sailed?"

"Nothing easier. I'll send a note to Captain Forbes at once."

"Very good, sir. Then I'll decide. Of course, I'll not act on my own. I'll get Braund to gather them in officially. He can do it through the killing of the Brown Priest. I can state positively that they were previously connected with him."

"Use your own methods. It will be a relief to know that they are rounded up though how they knew so much I can't imagine."

"I am more certain than ever that there has been a leakage from someone very close to you."

Half an hour later, Rushton was poring over a wad of flimsies, copies of wireless messages received since the *Corsair* sailed from Southampton.

He was able to discard the majority after only a brief glance for they were no more than 'bon voyage' wishes to the recipients from friends or relatives left behind.

One or two were business messages in plain English which seemed innocent enough. Then Rushton came to one that caused him to ponder.

It was from Paris and in French and was addressed to Count de Saladier. A rough translation ran something as follows:

"Hope everything all right expect your good news earliest opportunity the hawk has flown from Paris to Cherbourg."

It was signed 'Jean' which told Rushton nothing at all, nor could he fathom, at the moment, what was meant by that cryptic reference to a hawk.

He laid it aside for the time being and continued his task. After several more discards, he found another that caught his attention. It had been handed in at Cherbourg and, again, was addressed to the Saladiers. It said simply: "The hawk has alighted." It bore no name of the sender.

The 'hawk' again. He was getting intrigued in earnest now.

The next one that engaged his attention was in Spanish and had been handed in at Bordeaux. It was addressed to 'Senor Jose Ricardo' and ran:

"Sailing to-night all well rendezvous as arranged."

It was not signed. But Rushton studied it more closely than the others. It was harmless enough on the face of it. It seemed to be no more than a message from one person to another, both of whom were sailing in different ships.

He laid it aside and then, after further discards, reached the message that, he knew from the time indicated, must be the one that had been handed to the Saladiers while he was with them. It was from London and read:

"The eagle flies with the hawk they nest on the same branch."

Grant Rushton finished the few remaining flimsies and then, lighting a cigarette, began to pace the room.

Now and then his lips moved as if he were forming words but no sound came. Had those words been voiced, however, they would have been distinguished as follows:

"The hawk and the eagle—the hawk and the eagle—the eagle flies with the hawk—they nest on the same branch. But the eagle is not mentioned until this message that arrived this morning—from London. The hawk flew from Paris. The hawk alighted at Cherbourg. Yet the eagle— by heavens, I've got it! Years ago, when Sir Charles was a skipper himself, he had a reputation on all the seven seas. The eagle, that's what they used to call him. And, if he is the eagle then I must be the hawk. It fits, it fits like a glove. And this message came from London. I told him there was treachery there. Someone in his own office is the traitor. They have just discovered that he is on board and have tipped off the Saladiers. All right, I'll show them that the hawk can soar."

The fog that had cleared early in the morning, came down in a thick blanket at mid-day. It was like night. Even with the lights going full on in the saloons there was a haze penetrating everywhere that shrouded even nearby objects. The siren kept up a steady dirge.

In a much less luxurious suite than was occupied by Grant Rushton, three persons sat in close confab.

They were the Count and Countess de Saladier and a man of slim but athletic build, swarthy skin and the smoky brown eyes of the born killer, though the average observer would not have seen that unless they should be turned full upon him in open menace. Usually, Andre Bernaud was regarded as a somewhat stupid, sleepy sort of fellow, too lazy to take much interest in anything but the pocket sketch-book without which he was seldom seen.

But the eyes were not sleepy now. They were fixed full upon the 'Orchid' who, reclining on the couch with a cigarette, was speaking.

"It is a thing very mysterious," she was saying in French. "Who has seen him since he went last night to the suite of this Monsieur Rushton? He was to return and inform us of the result of that visit. He has not come. Nor have you, Andre, been able to find him. Yet we see the Monsieur Rushton on deck this morning. I tell you again, something has gone amiss."

"If he has betrayed us," began the killer; but the woman cut him short.

"Don't be a fool. The Brown Priest is no traitor. Jean and I have worked with him too often. If anything is wrong it is not of his doing. And now we need him. This message from Frick in London—it tells us that Sir Charles Gilson himself is on board. And we have proved that to be so. You have located him, Andre. He is in the suite next to Monsieur Rushton. But where is the Brown Priest? Has Rushton done something to him? I say I am uneasy. He should be here. What do you think, Jean?"

She turned to her husband who was stroking his beard thoughtfully.

"I agree with you, my dear," he said slowly. "Something has happened to the Brown Priest. He would not stay away so long. And now that we know Monsieur Gilson himself is on board everything is altered. But if we must act without him then let us do so. We shall wait until tonight. If the Brown Priest has not appeared we shall carry out the plan without him. I think Rushton is suspicious. It places things in our hands now that we know Monsieur Gilson is on board. We shall deal first with Rushton; then for the other. You will be ready, Andre?"

The killer shrugged.

"Am I not always ready?"

The 'Orchid' was about to speak again when, suddenly, there came a low tap at the door. All three looked at each other swiftly, then the 'Orchid' nodded almost imperceptibly at Bernaud. The killer slipped a gun out of an armpit holster and, holding it against his hip, stepped softly to the door.

He unlocked it and opened it an inch or so. The first thing he saw was the rough material of a monk's robe, brown in colour. Instantly he drew the door wider.

"Voilà," he said to the two behind him, "here he is now. We have been waiting for you, *mon vieux—mon dieu!*"

The exclamation burst from him as the business end of a pistol was pushed into his ribs.

"Quite so," came the rasping voice of Rushton. "Drop that gun—quick."

Bernaud, the killer, caught napping for the first time in his whole career of crime, hesitated. He was quick as lightning with a gun and he was debating swiftly what his chances were of flinging up the weapon and pouring a stream of lead into the bulk in front of him.

But Grant Rushton jammed the muzzle in harder.

"Quick, I said," he snarled, "drop it or I'll rub you out where you stand. And you two," he added to the Saladiers, "sit just as you are."

Bernaud let the gun fall with a thud to the carpet. Rushton prodded him farther into the cabin and, with his free hand, frisked him expertly for further guns, still keeping half an eye on the 'Orchid' who still reclined on the couch as if the visit was quite ordinary.

But Rushton mistrusted her and well was it for him that he did so. One moment she was utterly relaxed, watching him from under half lowered lids. The next she had sprung up in an incredibly swift leap, one hand holding her bag while the other tore it open.

In the same moment the count also came into action and, sensing what was going on behind him, Bernaud stiffened to spring.

But Rushton felt him tense. Like lightning his left fist caught Bernaud full on the chin, sending him back and down with a crash.

Then Rushton leaped for the 'Orchid,' grasping her wrist just as she dragged a gun out of the bag.

He swung her round with brutal force and held her despite her struggles while he kept the count covered with the gun.

"That will be about enough," he snapped. "Hold it as it is or someone is going to get hurt."

"As you have dealt with the Brown Priest," panted the 'Orchid,' still struggling.

Although the words were ignored by Rushton at the time, he was to recall them later. But now he had other things to attend to. Dragging the woman with him, he backed to the door and turned his head a little.

"All right," he called so that his voice went along the passage.

There followed the tramp of feet in step and then appeared the uniformed figures of Commander Braund followed by one of his officers and a file of half a dozen armed men.

"It is as I told you," remarked Rushton curtly. "That fellow on the floor pulled a gun on me. It is there where he dropped it. The woman's gun is by the couch. You will probably find the count armed as well. I turn them over to you, Commander."

He released the woman who flung round upon him like a fury. But, at sight of the stolid guard, she shrugged and reached for her cigarette case.

"I don't know the meaning of this outrage," she said coolly, "but I protest strongly against such treatment. There will be more heard of this."

"They will need a sharp eye kept on them," was what Rushton said to the Commander, ignoring her. "Will you carry on now?"

"We shall see that they are well taken care of until we reach Las Palmas," was the reply.

Rushton nodded and slipped his gun away. Then he passed out and started briskly along the corner.

He was more than satisfied with the swift coup he had effected. It had been impossible to make an open arrest only on the suspicions he held.

It had been necessary to secure something more definite and he had got it. Now they were off his hands. They would be kept well guarded until the ship made her next port, and that meant that Sir Charles could come out into the open.

His job was done, and well done at that. It would please Sir Charles. He would go along quite openly and tell him that the danger was over.

He traversed the corridors and went up by the staircase to the deck above on which his own suite was situated.

There was no need now to reach Sir Charles by way of the secret panel in the bathroom. He strode boldly along until he came to the branch passage leading down to Sir Charles's suite.

He rapped on the door confidently and stood waiting. At first no answering sound came from within. He rapped again and then a frown gathered as an odd noise reached his ears.

He bent his head so that his ear was close to the panel. Again the sound reached him, an indistinct, gurgling sound.

More puzzled than ever, Rushton turned the handle and found that the door yielded readily.

He pushed it open and then he stood on the threshold, appalled at the scene before him.

CHAPTER VII

IT looked as if a cyclone had struck the place.

Whatever furniture wasn't clamped to the floor had been overturned. Drawing materials were scattered about as if someone had leapt upon them in a frenzy.

A bottle of ink was smashed against one wall, leaving a sprawling stain. The silk curtains over the windows were hanging in ribbons. The french window was open, the shutters swinging loosely.

But the wreckage of the place itself was nothing to what lay in the chaotic setting.

One man lay sprawled on the floor, his head on a great stain that Rushton knew was blood. A little later he found that it was Green.

A second lay half in, half out of the french window, one leg bent oddly. It was Follet.

But what sent Rushton leaping across the room was a third figure, lying flat on its face, spread-eagled. One glance was enough to show him that it was Sir Charles Gilson.

He turned him over and found he was breathing. Getting to his feet he sprang to the bell. He met the steward at the door.

"Listen, you," he said sharply, "bring the doctor here at once. Tell him it is of the utmost urgency. Make haste."

He had held the door so the man could not see inside the cabin. Now he closed it and shot the bolt. He made for the sideboard and poured out some brandy.

The sound he had heard when standing outside came again. He saw now that it was Sir Charles, groaning.

He tried to get some of the spirit between his lips, but it only slopped over. Setting the glass down, he opened the door of the sleeping chamber and sped to the bathroom. He noticed as he went through that there appeared to have been no disturbance here.

He was bathing Sir Charles's temples when a knock came at the door. He admitted the doctor, who gazed dumbfounded at the scene.

"What on earth has happened here, Mr. Rushton?"

"I don't know. This is what I found when I arrived. Will you look at the others, Doctor? I believe Sir Charles is coming round."

The other nodded and went first to Green. A few moments only were enough to enable him to give his verdict there.

"He's dead," he muttered. "Shot clean between the eyes—instantaneous."

He knelt over Follet and found that he too, was past aid. A bullet had plunged into his heart.

He joined Rushton, who had pointed to the side of Sir Charles's head.

"A bullet creased him there," he jerked.

"Whoever plugged him thought he had got him. But it did little more than stun him. He's coming round now. Shall we try and get some of that brandy down him?"

"Yes, hold him like that while I try."

This time, they managed to get the semiconscious man to swallow some of the brandy. He choked, sputtered and tried to sit up.

Rushton held him with an arm about his shoulders.

"It's all right, sir," he kept assuring him. "You'll be better in a few moments."

"Better—I'm better now," mumbled the game old fellow. "Let me get at those blighters and— where's Green—and Follet?"

"They got it worse than you did, sir," Rushton told him frankly. He knew it would serve no purpose to dissemble with Sir Charles when the two others lay dead before his eyes. "Take it easy for a bit."

"It's you, is it, Rushton? Help me up. Where's Forbes? Get Captain Forbes here."

Rushton and the doctor got Sir Charles to his feet. Rushton rang for the steward again and sent a message to Captain Forbes. Then he slid out of the brown monk's robe. He saw the doctor helping Sir Charles into the inner cabin.

They persuaded him to lie on the bed while the doctor dressed the wound on the side of his head. But the indomitable old fellow was impatient for him to finish.

"You were too late," he said to Rushton. "You should have acted sooner."

"But I did act, sir," said Rushton quickly. "I did just as I told you I would do. I caught them together and backed them down with a gun. Then I turned them over to Commander Braund. They are under arrest now."

"Then how the devil did they get us?" demanded Sir Charles. "Never mind, we'll discuss this presently. Who is that?"

It was Commander Braund looking for Rushton.

"Captain Forbes can't leave the bridge just now," he announced. "What has happened, sir?"

Rushton drew back and listened to what Sir Charles had to say. His pointed white beard was working truculently while he talked.

"I was in here," he said, "when I thought I saw something in the fog out on the balcony. I passed so swiftly I couldn't be sure. Then I heard sounds in the outer cabin where Green and Follet were working. I opened the door and found them held up by a masked figure. They were game. They defied the blackguard's gun so as to save the plans, and there was a pitched fight. I don't think the intruder wanted to shoot for fear of attracting attention, though, when he did shoot the gun didn't make much noise— silencer. I rushed in to help but he got me with a bullet. That's all I remember. Of course the plans arc gone. Rushton says he rounded up the gang we suspected. If they didn't do it, then who the devil did? We'll comb this ship from stem to stern, Braund. Get that murderer, and get him soon."

"I'll report to the captain at once, sir."

The Commander glanced at Rushton who shook his head.

"I want to speak to Sir Charles alone," he said.

"No time to waste here," snapped Sir Charles. "There must be more of that gang running loose."

"I've got something to tell you."

"Very well," agreed the other. "Leave us, will you?"

The Commander and doctor withdrew, closing the door. Then Rushton sat down on the side of the bed and began to talk in low tones.

A quarter of an hour passed before he came out. He found Captain Forbes waiting, a harassed expression on his weather-beaten face.

"Go in now, will you, Captain? He wants to see you."

The other glanced at him keenly.

"This is terrible, Mr. Rushton. What do you make of it?"

Rushton shook his head.

"I don't know. But see Sir Charles. He's in a great state."

With that, Rushton opened the door and stepped into the passage. He walked slowly along to his own suite and went in, slamming the door after him with great force.

Lighting a cigarette he sat down, his face moody. He was in the same position when, a few minutes later, a loud voice could be heard in the passage outside.

"Where is he? Where is he, I say? I've got something to say to him."

With that, the door was flung open revealing Sir Charles Gilson as the one who had been shouting. Behind him was Captain Forbes, trying to soothe him. And, back of him again was the doctor.

"So there you are," cried Sir Charles. "A devil of a nice mess you've made of things. What have you got to say for yourself?"

Rushton rose, frowning as if it were an effort to restrain a hot retort.

"You have already said that, Sir Charles," he protested. "Why repeat it?"

"Why repeat it? You've got a nerve asking that after making a mess of things. And all you can do is to sit here smoking. I'm finished with you, do you understand? You are no longer acting for me. You can go ashore at Las Palmas and get what money is coming to you in London. Frick warned me that you were no good, said he wouldn't put it past you to sell out if someone offered you enough, and by heavens, I wouldn't be surprised if you had done it. There's been something crooked that needs some explaining."

"I've done nothing crooked," blazed Rushton. "If you listen to Frick you'll listen to anything. Did you expect me to wet nurse you every moment? I'm sick of your accusations. I haven't sold you out, but, by heavens, I wish now I'd had the chance. I'd teach you to hand me talk like that. I'll clear out at Las Palmas all right, but, until then, leave me alone. If I'm no longer in your employ I'm entitled to be free of your insults. This is my suite even if you are the owner of the ship, and I'll be obliged if you'll leave me alone."

"By heavens, for two pins I'd have you put under arrest."

"You can't do it. You'd be better under arrest yourself. If you try any tricks on me, I'll make a case in court that will fix your luxury cruises for you."

In the midst of these shouted recriminations, Captain Forbes managed to persuade Sir Charles to listen to him.

"Don't get yourself worked up like this, sir. You're still in no condition to do so. I beg you to come away. Say no more, Mr. Rushton. I command you to refrain from exciting Sir Charles further or I will put you under arrest."

"Then let him take his insults away," snapped Rushton. "I'm fed up with his accusations."

Between them, the captain and doctor got Sir Charles along the passage. Rushton closed the door with a slam and bolted it noisily. Then he went to the sideboard and poured himself a drink.

When he had downed that, he got into a loose overcoat and cap, lit a fresh cigarette and unbolted the door.

"Even fog will be a relief after that," he muttered as he closed the door, no longer taking pains to lock it.

His face was so stern that it invited no approach from those he passed. Had the 'Orchid' seen him then her eyes would have been more mocking than ever, for his discomfiture would have given her great joy.

But she was safely under guard in her own suite, and, at first, Rushton had the fog-enveloped deck to himself as he strode moodily along.

He found a place at the rail and leant over, below him he could just make out the water close to the ship as it broke in a stream of foam.

No one else seemed to be about. The wet fog had driven them to the more attractive surroundings of the saloons.

Nevertheless, someone else was abroad on the deck for, while Rushton still stood leaning against the rail, a light footstep sounded behind him, then it paused and, as a tentative voice spoke his name, he turned to see the girl he had met as Mrs. Rentley's companion.

How could she, or anyone else, know that he and Sir Charles had been playing a part?

CHAPTER VIII

HE could just see her smiling at him shyly.

"So you're another who doesn't mind the fog," he hazarded as she stood at the rail beside him.

"I don't mind the fog but I hate the dirge of the siren. I'm afraid I'm not a very good sailor."

"You'll soon get your sea legs. Lots of people find it a bit difficult the first day or two out."

"I did, but I'm better now. I had better confess though that it wasn't the fog that brought me out on deck."

"A confession? Why do you say that?"

"I—I really followed you out."

"That is most flattering."

He looked straight down into her eyes. She returned his gaze for a moment, then her eyes dropped.

"I didn't mean it that way," she returned, speaking quickly. "I'm afraid I'm getting this all muddled. I really came on behalf of Mrs. Rentley."

He laughed.

"I shan't misunderstand you," he told her. "But why did Mrs. Rentley send you to find me?"

"I hope you won't think that we were eavesdropping but it was impossible not to hear—to hear—"

He laughed again.

"You mean you overheard the altercation that took place in my suite a few minutes ago?"

"Yes."

"That's too bad. I'm afraid I lost my temper badly. But I was tried severely. However, I've cooled off now. I expect I shall make an apology and that will be the end of it. I shall get off the ship at the first opportunity."

"I'm awfully sorry. I don't know anything about it and don't want to know but I feel you would not have been so upset unless you had cause."

"That is very nice of you but I'm afraid I have the devil of a temper when it gets hold of me. I'm out of a job over it anyway."

"That is why Mrs. Rentley sent me to find you. I don't know what she wants but she said to ask you if you would come and see her."

"I don't mind seeing her but I can't imagine what she can want. When does she want me to go?"

"Now if you will."

"All right. Will you take me down?"

"Yes."

He looked into her eyes again but in them he could detect no subterfuge. If her shyness was a cloak then she was no mean actress.

He did not ask her further what Mrs. Rentley could want. He signed that he was ready to go and they turned towards the entrance to the saloon lobby.

At the door of Mrs. Rentley's suite, he waited while the girl knocked and opened the door. When she did so, he saw the old lady sitting in an easy chair with some knitting in her hands. She smiled a welcome as she saw him.

"Come in, Mr. Rushton, come in. You can go, my dear," she added to the girl. "I'll send for you later."

The girl murmured something and went out, closing the door. Mrs. Rentley motioned Rushton to the other easy chair. He sat down and accepted a cigarette from the box that she took from the table. Then he waited.

"What has Cara told you?" she asked abruptly.

"Just that you wished to see me."

"Did she say that we had overheard something of the altercation that took place in your cabin?"

"Yes. I am sorry if I disturbed you. But I was very angry."

"We all get angry," she said with a nod. "Was it as serious as it sounded?"

"Quite."

Suddenly she tossed the knitting aside and lit a cigarette. Her movements were no longer those of a fumbling old woman. Her eyes were fixed very alertly on Rushton.

"Are you, then, completely finished in the work you were doing?"

"I am out of a job, if that is what you mean."

"What are you going to do?"

"Return to England by the first chance, I suppose, but I'd—"

"You'd what?"

"Oh, nothing. I don't suppose it does any good to harbour revengeful thoughts."

"But you do feel that way."

He was silent for a few moments, glowering at the floor. Then he burst out harshly.

"I'm no angel. I don't want to talk too much but I've had a raw deal. No one knows how hard I've worked for a certain man and then, just because things go wrong, I'm bawled out in public and expected to take it. I won't do it. I've never had such treatment. But I'll get my own back some way. I'm not going to take it lying down."

"For whom were you working then?"

He looked at her in surprise.

"Oh, I forgot. Of course you wouldn't know. I was working for Sir Charles Gilson, the owner of this line. But I can't tell you what I was doing."

"Perhaps I know what you were doing. We will discuss that presently. But tell me, how would you like an opportunity to get even with him for his treatment of you? I want a straight answer to that. I want to know just how seriously you feel about it."

"A chance to get even with him? I'd do anything to get my own back on that old devil. He's treated me like a dog."

She rose and went to the door, bolting it. Then she returned to her chair and, sitting down, looked Rushton in the eye.

"If you mean that," she said in a low tone, "then I can put you in the way to have your revenge many times over. But I've got to be convinced of your sincerity."

He seemed bewildered.

"I don't know how I am to convince you of my sincerity. But I do mean what I said."

"You can prove your sincerity very easily."

"How?"

"By telling me, a perfect stranger, what was the nature of your work for Sir Charles Gilson." He hesitated.

"It was of a very secret nature, but that doesn't matter now. He, himself, made it public enough to-day. I owe nothing to him any longer. I don't mind telling you what it was."

"What was it?"

"Sir Charles Gilson had some plans covering a very important series of inventions relating to a floating aerodrome that is to be moored in the South Pacific. Have you read anything about it?"

"I have read about such a drome."

"Well, it is on its way out there now. It is being towed by two tugs. The drome itself isn't so much but there has always been great difficulty in devising some means of safe mooring and a method of smooth landing for planes. Those plans of Sir Charles's cover those difficulties. They mean a huge fortune to the person who possesses them. Several people have been after them and it was my job to guard them and Sir Charles. Well, to-day, I thought I had discovered the gang that was after them. I held them up in their suite and placed them under arrest. But, while I was busy there, other persons got into Sir Charles's suite, killed his two confidential engineers who were working on the plans and nearly killed Sir Charles. They got away with the plans. That is why he sacked me."

"I see. Did you know anything about the details of these plans?"

"Oh, yes, I know how they were to be applied."

"Then you must be one of the few still alive who would know that?"

"Probably the only one except Sir Charles himself."

"You have been very frank with me, Mr. Rushton, but I can assure you that I shall respect your confidence. I have some things to say to you but not just yet. Will you come and see me again this evening?"

"If you wish, but I don't quite see—"

"Of course you don't. But you will understand later. I have an offer to make you—I think."

He rose.

"At what time shall I come?"

"Shall we say nine o'clock?"

"I shall be here. You are very kind."

With that, he left. He went into his own suite for a few minutes and then again sought the deck.

The freakish fog was again lifting and, already, visibility was much better. Rushton paced the promenade alone. He found himself hoping that Miss Hume would put in an appearance, but she did not do so.

He passed the sleek looking South American on his way to the smoke saloon, but no salutation passed between them. He was still there when the dressing bugle went just after sunset. At the moment, Rushton was standing forward, gazing over the leaden sea that now was comparatively smooth after the earlier turmoil.

Far ahead, over the port bow, he could see another ship steaming on the same course. But she did not appear to have anything like the speed of the *Corsair* for, during the half hour or so before dusk shut her from view, he could see that the *Corsair* was overtaking fast.

He changed perfunctorily and dined at a small table in the restaurant alone. He spoke to no one and no one spoke to him with the exception of Commander Braund who passed close. But then no more than a curt nod passed between the two men.

Along towards eight o'clock, Mrs. Rentley came in alone and sat at a table some distance from Rushton. She was not looking his way so he did not attempt to speak to her. He did not see Cara Hume, and wondered if she were again feeling seedy. Then he reflected that perhaps Mrs. Rentley did not care to have her dine at the same time.

He was back in his own suite before a quarter to nine and smoked there until nine. Prompt to the minute, he stepped across the corridor and knocked on the door of the opposite suite.

A voice bade him enter. He found Mrs. Rentley sitting in the same chair she had occupied during the afternoon. He noticed that one of the french windows was ajar, letting in a current of cool air.

She asked him to bolt the door. He did so and then sat down waiting. She looked at him for a few moments in silence.

"I've been thinking about things," she said abruptly, "and I have decided to make you an offer."

He inclined his head but said nothing.

"I'm going to make a disclosure that may or may not be unwise on my part but it won't make any difference. I shall take care that it has no untoward results for myself. Do you still mean what you said this afternoon?"

"Yes."

"You would place yourself at the disposal of interests that are working against Sir Charles Gilson?"

"I would under certain conditions."

"What conditions?"

"That it proved profitable to me."

"That would be taken for granted. Your profit would be enormous."

"Do I understand that I am to receive such a proposition from you?"

"Yes. No one is in a better position to make you such an offer for it was I who took those plans."

"You!"

Rushton gazed at her in open astonishment.

"Yes. But just so you won't change your mind and decide you'd like to take them from me, I had better add that they are no longer on board this ship."

"I am entirely bewildered."

"I want you to wait here for just a few moments."

As she spoke, she rose and vanished into the inner cabin. Rushton smoked and waited. She reappeared very soon and, as he turned his head, he came to his feet in fresh amazement.

It was not Mrs. Rentley. It was a young woman with close-cropped black hair and a lithe, well-formed figure that was clad in a one-piece black bathing suit. Over this hung a rag of a red silk dressing robe.

But the voice was a clearer, younger rendering of that which Mrs. Rentley had used. And he noticed that, in one hand, she carried a pistol that was fitted with a silencer.

"Now we'll talk plainly," she said briskly. "Sit down and listen to me."

He obeyed. She took the other chair. Then she indicated the pistol.

"I'll use this you know, if necessary, and I shan't make a mistake this time."

"Then it was you who shot at me when I first came aboard."

"Of course. I didn't know you would be wearing a bullet-proof garment. But never mind. It is well that I didn't get you. We can be useful to each other."

"It looks as though we might," he agreed.

"The Saladier gang didn't get the plans," she went on. "I saw to that. And I had my eye on you every moment. I wanted to bring a crisis between you and them so as to leave my own hands free. That is why the Brown Priest was found at your door."

"You did that then?"

"I did."

"And took the letter that was pushed under the door?"

"Yes. It was all very easy. You see I found it simple to reach your cabin by way of the balcony. I have been a circus acrobat since a child. I have had free access to your suite whenever I wished. And everything went just as I planned. You went for the Saladier gang. They thought it was you who killed the Brown Priest. In the mix-up I got the plans."

"And killed the two engineers."

She snapped her fingers.

"Pouf! That was necessary. This is not child's play. We are after big stakes. And you would have killed just as quickly."

"How do you know that I won't take those plans away from you?"

"For two reasons. The first is because I'll shoot you dead if you make a move against me. The second is that the plans are no longer on board this ship."

"You said that before."

"You do not believe me? You are foolish to think I would bluff at a time like this. The plans were taken by Ricardo when he went with the girl."

Rushton knew he was getting the truth. She seemed to feel so sure of him that she was not attempting to hedge.

"You have worked fast."

"I don't muddle things when I handle them. That is why I am paid highly. And I'm not in the least afraid of telling you just what has happened. You have failed. You have quarrelled with Sir Charles. You say you are not averse to getting your own back. If you want to come in with me, I can use you. As I say, we have the plans but we are not in a position to apply them immediately. You say you know what should be done. Therefore I make you an offer. Come in with me and, not only will you get your own back but you will touch a very handsome reward."

"How much?"

"Say fifty thousand pounds."

"And further work when this job is done?"

"If you make good, yes."

"Then I'm your man. What is the next step?"

"To leave this ship to-night. We shall be picked up by the other ship."

"What is that?"

"Ever hear of the Ship of the Accursed?"

"Of course."

"She's less than two miles away from us at this moment. She was ahead this afternoon but dropped back as soon as it became dark. She was not going ahead at her full speed. Ricardo and the girl have already gone."

"Ricardo, so he is your accomplice."

"How did you know?"

"He was waiting for that book in which you had written a message on the flyleaf."

She studied him with fresh interest.

"You're cleverer than I thought."

"So your companion is in this too?"

"Not she. She was only a blind to help my pose as a silly old woman. But Ricardo has taken a fancy to her. He wants to take her on to South America for his amusement. She didn't know she was going until he took her over the side with him an hour ago."

Grant Rushton knew what fate would be the girl's when the man Ricardo grew tired of her and abandoned her in South America, the worst white slave pool on earth.

"Over the rail," he said slowly. "Is that how we go?"

"Yes. Are you game?"

"When do we start?"

She glanced at the electric clock in the wall.

"In exactly ten minutes. You haven't much time to make up your mind."

"It is made up. I go."

She stood up, a vital, supple figure in the close-fitting suit.

"I'm glad," she told him. "If you had refused now I should have had to kill you and, for some reason, I don't want to do that any longer. Is there anything you want to bring— pocket articles?"

"No. I go just as I am."

"Then come out on to the balcony. We must be ready."

The hands of the clock pointed to exactly half past nine when, one after the other, two figures dropped from the private balcony of Mrs. Rentley's suite into the water.

No one saw them. They were just two bobbing specks left swiftly behind as the great luxury liner, ablaze with light, raced on through the night.

A blue light flared up from the face of the sea.

It rose, spreading narrowly like a stream from a nozzle. Then it died down and vanished.

The two who floated within the circle of lifebuoys waited. In one direction the lights of the *Corsair* were gone. In every other direction there was nothing.

A second time that blue streak stabbed the night and again it died away. Calcium flares. The woman spoke.

"Two, that was the signal agreed upon. They ought to be within sight. Watch carefully."

Rushton did not answer. He was twisting his head this way and that searching across the waste of waters. Then, suddenly, he saw a light unmasked. It did not seem a great distance away, perhaps a mile or so, though under such conditions distance was most difficult to guess.

"Do you see that?" he called.

Her voice came back to him.

"Yes. They will put a boat out at once. We'll give them a certain time and then I'll send another light up."

They rode the swell easily enough though Rushton was worried a little about the risk of the fog descending again. An age passed. They said nothing. Both were waiting and watching. Then, suddenly, the blue flame hissed skywards once more.

Scarcely had it died away when, from across the water, there came an answering flare. When it was gone, the woman called to Rushton.

"Shout to them, your voice will carry farther than mine."

Rushton obeyed. Lifting his voice he bellowed mightily across the water. Then, in the distance, there was an answering shout. Rushton waited a few minutes and then sent another hail. The answer came closer this time.

The woman sent still another signal flare into the sky and then it seemed no time before they were both shouting directions to the boat that was approaching.

A ship's lifeboat appeared out of the gloom. The woman and Rushton were hauled in. Rushton could not see faces distinctly but he thought he recognised that of the man he had known as Ricardo on board the *Corsair*.

He and Mrs. Rentley began talking at once in low tones. No one gave any orders. The crew pulled as they willed and, as far as Rushton could make out, seemed to be a scratch, undisciplined lot.

He thought it likely that the woman was telling Ricardo about him. He did not attempt to overhear. He lay back in his seat watching the lights of the other ship as they drew nearer and nearer.

They bumped in against an accommodation ladder, and when the woman had gone up Ricardo touched Rushton on the arm.

"You go next," he said curtly.

Rushton obeyed. The moment he stepped over the side he saw that the Ship of the Accursed had been well named. Never had his eyes rested upon such a collection of ruffians as met his gaze now.

That part of the deck which he could see would have broken the heart of the most slipshod sailor. It was littered with all sorts of gear and packed with men lying, sprawling, squatting or standing as the mood took them.

Several arc lights had been slung aloft so as to illuminate the deck from stem to stern. A cask of what Rushton guessed to be either rum or cheap wine stood braced at one side and there was a constant line of men coming from it or going to it, each with a dipper or cup in his hand.

Half a dozen games of chance were in progress. One crowd was quarrelling with a profanity that shocked even the hard-boiled Rushton. The quarrel broke with amazing swiftness into desperate action.

Two men sprang to their feet. Rushton saw the flash of a knife. But before the blade could reach its mark there was the bark of a pistol. The knife man dropped in his tracks. His murderer snarled a word to a companion. The pair picked up the dead man and went through his pockets with rough hands. Then they swung him over the side and sat down again to their game. No one seemed to pay any more than the most casual attention. It was a valuable object lesson to Rushton.

Ricardo was smiling cynically. Mrs. Rentley had disappeared. Ricardo spoke curtly again.

"Come along. You are wanted in the saloon."

They picked their way aft among the lounging criminals. Some of them paid not the slightest attention. Others stared at Rushton with evil grins. It was the worst hell-hole into which Rushton had ever stepped.

They descended the after companion and came into a large saloon, dirty, littered and full of smoke. And, despite the fact that he was being sponsored by Mrs. Rentley and, for the moment, had been taken in hand by Ricardo, Rushton found himself regarded with veiled suspicion and hostility by those who were gathered round the table. Mrs. Rentley was already among them. He guessed that she had told them about him. Ricardo dropped into a vacant seat. Rushton was left standing.

He swept them with a cool stare. There were three besides Mrs. Rentley and Ricardo.

One was a big blond man with a face of granite. Rushton had seen him before—in London, Paris, Berlin, elsewhere. He had always suspected him of being a *chevalier d'industrie*. Now he knew the truth. He learned a little later that he was a German working for the same interests in the Argentine by whom Ricardo, indeed the whole gang was employed.

The other two were, he discovered, Dutch. They were very similar in appearance and extremely well dressed as, indeed, was the German.

He found they were brothers bearing a name he had heard whispered more than once when some big international coup was impending. He had seen enough already to get some idea of the real strength of the gang he had joined. There was no doubt that they were far more powerful and much better equipped financially than the Saladier gang.

While he stood under their cold scrutiny, he was introduced by Mrs. Rentley who, despite her sex, seemed to speak with a certain tone of authority to which the others deferred, outwardly at least.

Had Sir Charles Gilson realised into what Rushton would plunge when he suggested his daring subterfuge he never for a moment would have listened or consented. Even Rushton himself felt a queer sensation run down his spine as he stood up to the battery of those suspicious eyes.

It was the German who spoke first. Rushton had seen him looking at Mrs. Rentley. There seemed to be some sort of understanding between them but Rushton could not guess what it was although he had a strong suspicion that it concerned him.

"I think," said the German in very bad English, "I think we ask you to retire for a little. We talk and then we have you back. You agree?"

Rushton made a curt gesture of assent.

"As you will. You know why I am here. It seems to me that the less time we waste the better."

The German was about to speak again, but the door leading to the companion opened and a fellow whom Rushton knew must be one of the six hundred criminals entered.

He was a big, murderous-looking ruffian who leered at the assembled group familiarly. His clothes were little better than rags, his face hadn't known a razor for weeks, he stank of spirits.

Around his waist was a strong leather belt and to this was attached a long knife, two pistols and what looked like a rusty knuckleduster.

He leant up against the jamb of the door and spat out a squirt of tobacco juice that sailed past Mrs. Rentley's shoulder with no more than inches to spare.

Rushton felt a quick admiration for her. She didn't turn a hair, just glanced at the fellow and turned back to the table.

But for all the hostility that was electric in the saloon, not one of those at the table attempted to put the fellow in his place. They waited until, still smiling evilly, he turned to lounge out again.

It was then his eyes met Rushton's gaze fully. He stared for a moment with a peculiar expression just flickering in them before he turned away.

But that moment was enough to tell Rushton that the fellow had recognised him. They had met somewhere before. Where had it been? Where had he come up against this murdering jailbird in the past and under what circumstances? He knew that he must lose no time in stripping that brutal face of its beard and reconstruct the features beneath. Some instinct warned him that this development was going to be vital to him, one way or another.

But he had little time then to devote to that problem. Ricardo had got to his feet and now guided him along a passage to a small saloon where a dilapidated piano told Rushton it had been the music saloon when the *Santa Cruz* had known happier times.

There he was left to his own devices for the time being. He was standing by the battered piano, idly studying certain marks that looked like bullet scars and trying to remember where he had seen that bearded ruffian before when a sound caused him to turn round. He saw Cara Hume coming towards him.

She came swiftly. He saw that her face was drawn, her eyes heavy with fatigue and fear. His own face betrayed nothing of what he felt at seeing her. Eyes, eyes everywhere, and Grant Rushton knew that he must not falter ever so little, so perilous was his position.

"So it is you," she said in a strained way. "I—I did not think you would have come here."

"Why not?" he asked coolly. "You came, didn't you?"

"Oh! You must know I did not come of my own free will. I was tricked on the other ship and I was brought away by force. But you, I am told that you have joined these people."

"They told you the truth."

"But how could you do such a thing? I had clung to the hope that you would help me. I did not think you could be so treacherous."

"You would attribute virtues to me that I do not possess," he told her coldly. "I am an adventurer. I sell my services to the highest bidder."

"And I thought you so different," she blazed suddenly. Then her whole body trembled and she covered her face with her hands. "What am I to do? Is it nothing to you that I have been dragged into this place and am at the mercy of that man? We are of the same race. They will not listen to me. I have sworn that I will say nothing if they will let me go. But he only laughs. Won't you help me—please?"

"You excite yourself needlessly," said Rushton lightly. "No one will harm you, I am sure."

She looked at him, her eyes filled with contempt.

"And I thought you a decent honourable gentleman," she said slowly. "I was terribly mistaken. I did not know you were just a common blackguard."

Rushton bowed with a smile but made no answer. The girl still stared at him as if still unable to believe that he could be of such vile breed. But his cold smile still remained and, with a low cry of despair, she turned and rushed from the saloon.

Rushton took out a cigarette and lighted it.

"A most emotional nature," he said aloud. "She apparently hasn't a very high opinion of me."

At that moment the door opened and Mrs. Rentley appeared. She gave Rushton a curious look then smiled.

"You have not been alone," she said lightly.

The words told Rushton that his suspicions had been well founded. He and the girl had been spied upon. It had probably been a trap. He shrugged.

"Your companion was here," he answered. "I find her somewhat hysterical. Why do you encumber yourself with her? Surely she can be of no use now?"

She laughed and thrust her arm under his in a way that displayed more confidence than she had conceded before.

"As a matter of fact I let her know you were in here. It is not my wish that she came. I would have left her in the *Corsair*. But it was a concession to Ricardo. He is quite mad about her. Now come along with me. They want to talk to you again. And remember, I am your friend."

He looked down at her. For the first time he realised that she was a devilishly fascinating woman. And in her eyes he read a message that was meant only for himself. That, he told himself, might mean further complications unless he could twist it to his own purpose.

"Am I accepted then?" he asked her.

"For the present. It is up to you to convince them. I have taken the responsibility. See that you do not fail."

"I won't fail," he promised her.

He found the others sitting just as he had left them. The German was watching him with the cold eyes of a judge who had already tried him and passed sentence.

Rushton bore himself with cool sangfroid. This time he approached a seat. Mrs. Rentley sat beside him. Her swift gaze seemed to carry a message to Ricardo for he grinned in friendly fashion at Rushton. Rushton would have found infinite pleasure in squeezing his fat neck between both hands.

"We have been discussing matters," he heard the German saying. "It seems, from what madame says, that you can be useful to us. You will have an immediate opportunity of proving your value. If madame is mistaken it will be unfortunate for you. Do I make myself clear?"

"Perfectly. But it must be equally understood that I receive a proportionate share of any proceeds. I do not work for nothing."

"You will get your share. Now, attend to me. You are fully conversant with certain plans that have come into our possession?"

"Yes."

"We have already had an opportunity of examining them. These two members of our organisation"—and he indicated the two Dutchmen—"are qualified engineers. They have read the plans carefully. But there are certain features which are not clear. Can you explain them?"

"I should be able to do so. I am familiar with the plans."

"Wait here."

The German rose and Rushton could see now that he was even bigger than he had guessed, he moved erectly and with a springy step that stamped him as a man of swift action despite his bulk. Rushton knew he would probably be the most dangerous of the lot to reckon with. He was, he could see, a man to whom human life meant absolutely nothing.

He vanished into a cabin that led directly off the saloon. When he reappeared he carried in his hands the plans that Rushton had last seen in Sir Charles Gilson's suite in the *Corsair*. He sat down and laid them on the table.

Then, before he could speak again, the door opened and two men lurched in. Rushton saw that one was the same ruffian who had entered so unceremonially before. The other was a gigantic negro, coal-black and glistening with sweat. His features were the heavy type of either Martinique or Hayti.

In front of every man at the table, with the exception of Rushton, lay a heavy automatic pistol. So far, Rushton had not been entrusted with a weapon.

Both ruffians seemed well primed with liquor.

The place was filled with an offensive stench. The German eyed them coldly.

"What is it now?" he asked curtly.

It was the bearded fellow who spoke.

"Me and my mates want to know what's happening," he growled. "We want to see something. What about putting in to Las Palmas. We're getting tired of rolling up and down the sea. We were promised action and then a fair share. What about it?"

The buck nigger grinned and rolled his eyes.

"Yass," he rumbled, "dass right."

Rushton sat tight. He knew that things were in such a state on board that anything might blow up at any moment. He didn't know what promises had been made to the cargo of criminals to induce them to agree to take a hand in any devilry that was going, but it was perfectly plain that they were held by a very weak thread and that they might get out of hand any time.

Nothing worse than that hell-ship could have been imagined. On the one hand were those six hundred odd creatures who were the sweepings of the criminal sewers of South America. On the other was the handful of men and one woman, equally criminal but using brain power rather than the bludgeon.

The arrangement that bound them together had nothing stable to hold it. If a blow-up came the result for the smaller party would be, to use the German's own expression, unfortunate.

Nevertheless the minority in the saloon remained cool enough. Rushton had to confess to himself that they were not lacking in courage, even the woman sat smiling fearlessly.

Then the German answered. He did not bluster. He did not pander. He spoke curtly and quietly, explaining that things were soon approaching a head and that, when they were over, there would be rich cut for everyone.

"Why are you so impatient?" he wound up. "You've got plenty to eat and plenty of liquor to drink. You are your own masters. When this thing is finished you get the ship and your cut. Then you can land where you want to."

The men seemed appeased, but there was something about the way the negro caressed the sharp edge of his knife that was all the more sinister for the wide smile on his face.

The bearded one growled something about telling his mates, then he spat tobacco juice on the door as if just to show that he was as good as anyone there.

His leer went round the table and, as it met Rushton's gaze, he winked deliberately. In a flash Rushton remembered where he had met the fellow before.

They lounged out and the German pushed the plans across to Rushton.

"You say you can read them. Prove it."

Rushton spread out the blue-prints. His lids were lowered so the others did not see the grim expression of his eyes as he saw the dark stains where blood had spattered.

His voice was curt and metallic when he indicated section after section, explaining briefly the purpose of each and how one was interrelated with the other.

Then, suddenly, he paused and frowned. He sat staring in silence while the others watched.

"What is it?" demanded the German sharply.

"Is this all?" asked Rushton.

"That is the packet just as I received it from madame."

"They are as I took them," she broke in. "What is it?"

"Wait."

Rushton turned them over and over. He checked and compared with meticulous care. Then he looked up.

"These are the plans," he drawled, "but—"

"But what?"

"They are quite useless as they stand."

"Why?"

"A part, the most vital part, the key section, is missing."

There was dead silence. All eyes were turned upon Mrs. Rentley. Rushton was also watching her. But he was not thinking about the plans. He was asking himself how it was that this woman, young and attractive enough, could be such a cold-blooded criminal, as careless of taking human life as the most hardened. What had been her earlier life? What had turned her into this? Or was she just a natural phenomenon! How could she discuss those killings so coolly?

"They are just as I took them," she was insisting. "I missed nothing. As soon as I finished off the three in that cabin I collected everything on the table. Are you sure the important part is missing?"

Rushton nodded. Until he had felt those plans in his own hands he had been thinking hard to find some way of continuing his bluff. The fact that the vital part was really missing gave him just the lead he needed. He knew he must play it very carefully and strongly.

"I am not mistaken. It is not here. I know the part well. It is that which concerns the system of automatic control that governs the floating drome in all weathers. I have heard Sir Charles Gilson say that the whole success of the thing hung on that. It may be that he considered it of such importance that he did not keep it attached to the rest of the plans, that he did not intend to produce it until his experts had actual need of it."

Someone cursed heavily. Mrs. Rentley was looking at Rushton.

"If you know the plans so well could you not supply the missing part?" she asked.

Rushton shook his head dubiously.

"I don't know. I am not an engineer. I know the general idea, of course. I can try, if you wish."

"If you know the idea you could explain to us and we could draw the designs," suggested the German.

Rushton agreed. He had gained what he had been working for—delay. But he did not know yet how he was going to apply it to his own advantage.

Nor was he going to get an opportunity then to discover for, from somewhere in the near distance, there came a sharp, agonising scream of terror that Rushton knew came from the throat of Cara Hume.

CHAPTER IX

DESPITE the urgent need to maintain at any cost the slight purchase he had gained upon this slippery ground of intrigue, Grant Rushton was on the point of throwing caution to the winds when that terror-stricken sound reached his ears.

He knew it was no devilry of Ricardo's that had caused the girl to scream. Ricardo was not crude. He would choose his own time and use more sophisticated methods.

Rushton did not know whether he had seen all the Rentley gang (as he termed them in his own mind) or if there might be others, of less importance, in other parts of the ship.

But he had already seen enough to convince him that the danger to a young and attractive girl in that hell-ship was one that might strike from hundreds of different directions. Briefly, nothing more perilous could be imagined.

His hand was already reaching for the nearest gun on the table when there came the sound of someone running hard. Next moment the door burst open and into the saloon rushed Cara Hume.

Her distress was pitiable. Her eyes were wide with terror, her face was like chalk and her throat was emitting short, agonised sounds of appeal for help.

And little wonder. At her heels came one of the most repulsive-looking ruffians Rushton had seen in many a day.

He was so short as to be almost a dwarf. The visible part of his body was thickly hirsute. His eyes were as redly evil as those of an ape. His mouth was a huge abyss showing two blackened stumps of teeth.

But what he lacked in height he made up in breadth. He was extraordinarily broad, with arms and legs as thick as tree-trunks. He wore only a pair of dirty dungarees and a filthy shirt. He was enough to strike terror to the heart of his brutal companions, let alone a girl so fresh and fastidious as Cara Hume.

The German had not moved. Like so many of his kind he regarded women as no more than so much baggage, although he was forced to docket Mrs. Rentley somewhat differently.

The two Dutchmen looked disturbed but did not rise. Mrs. Rentley had drawn back in disgust at sight of the brute, but could not have done anything even if she would.

Ricardo was the only one of the gang that showed active protest.

He scrambled to his feet and made as if to reach for a gun, but, long before his fingers could close upon it, Rushton had swung round his chair on its pivot and, just as the girl rushed past him, he rose. In doing so he brought his fist up with the whole lift of shoulder and body behind it, the whole thrust of hips and thighs too.

It connected with the dwarf's chin while he was leaping after the girl. His own impetus increased the effect of the impact. It was terrific. Short, heavy, bull-necked though he was, he was lifted clean off his feet and sent smashing over against the wall with a thud that shook the place.

He didn't rise. He lay there and Rushton wasn't the only one who knew that when he did rise again it would be when he was carried out. The crack of that neck breaking had been too distinct for mistake.

Rushton did not turn to the girl. He dared not do so. He knew he had already jeopardised the slight confidence he had inspired. He could only hope that they would think his action natural in one of his race.

But it needed all his restraint to keep his seat for, reaching the end of the saloon where she was forced to come to a halt, the girl turned to see the fate of her pursuer. She took one look. The reaction smote her! She slid to the floor in a dead faint.

Ricardo went to her and bent down. The German sneered with contempt. Mrs. Rentley smiled superciliously, though she turned warm eyes upon Rushton. It was not gratitude for what he had done. The fate of the girl was nothing to her. But she was the sort of woman who was stirred by that sort of prowess. And it may have occurred to her now and then that, despite the strength of her own position, she would find it quickly untenable if that drunken gang of worse than murderers turned.

Rushton was savage at having to sit and watch Ricardo paw Cara Hume. But if he had interfered now it would have been disastrous. Better to swallow the lesser than to choke on the greater.

But all of them needed their wits then for a fresh diversion. In through the same door by which the girl and her pursuer had arrived came two other ruffians.

By way of the companion there once more appeared the bearded fellow whom Rushton had succeeded in placing among the incidents of the past. On their heels was a rabble of a dozen or more. Things began to look really ugly.

There was no need to explain. There was the body of the fellow with a broken neck to speak for itself.

Rushton saw the German reach for his pistol. It looked as though matters were coming to a showdown before the main business of the compact had been attempted.

But the German wasn't going to permit the trifling discomfiture of a girl to upset his plans. Before any of the gang could speak he was on his feet.

"Listen to me," he snapped authoritatively. "Is this ship a place of bedlam or are we on a serious purpose? What the devil does it all mean, drinking and quarrelling and invading this place when I'm busy with plans? Haven't I told you that we are engaged upon a big thing? Are you such a gang of fools that you are going to wreck everything before we start? You have the run of the ship. I don't care about that. But I'm running this show and I'm going to have some sort of order. You," and he jabbed the barrel of the pistol towards the bearded fellow who seemed a sort of leader among the others, "you ought to have more sense at least."

"The men are getting fed up," he said sulkily.

"Fed up! Fed up with what? We haven't been aboard more than a week and you talk about being fed up. What about the months you've been roaming the seas? What about the times you've tried to land at port after port? You are pariahs that no one will have. And what have we offered you? We have offered you a chance to pick up money, plenty of it, if you behave yourselves. And now—this continual invasion."

But his words had little effect upon that gang. 'They were too seasoned with the life of the worst jails in South America to pay much heed to verbal admonition, even when there was such a cold eye behind it. Had the German dropped a couple of them in their tracks he would have accomplished one thing or the other—he would have precipitated a complete blow-up or he would have cowed them. Rushton had a hunch that such a stroke would have been a winner, but he sat tight, waiting. And then, suddenly, all attention was centred upon him. It was one of the fellows who had come in by the other door who pointed a dirty finger at him and snarled in the hybrid Portuguese of the Brazilian coast:

"There is the one who did it. He is the one. What does he do here? Why did he strike down my friend, Pedro?"

Others began to growl. Rushton knew that, if it came to the point, the German, the Dutchman and Ricardo would 'throw him to the wolves' without a qualm if it meant saving their own skin. Mrs. Rentley was an uncertain quantity.

Here, then, was a crisis with which he must deal himself. He came to his feet, weaponless. He walked quickly to the fellow who had singled him out for accusation. The fellow, remembering the shocking blow that had finished Pedro's career so suddenly, shrank back and began to claw out a knife.

But Rushton did not attack. Indeed, he did not seem to be paying any attention to the fellow. His gaze was fixed upon the bearded one who stood a little in advance of the rest.

"Take this fellow away," he snapped. "Are your wits so muddled that you do not know what you are doing?"

There was a growl from several throats. But instead of rising to the challenge, the bearded ruffian accepted the reproof with amazing docility.

He stepped forward and caught the shoulder of the one who was threatening Rushton.

"Come on out of it," he snarled. "Out, the lot of you. We'll give them a chance to keep their promise."

Despite murmurings, he had his way. Rushton paid them no more attention. He returned to his seat and again bent over the plans. But he was conscious all the time that several pairs of eyes were fixed upon him. And he knew the reason. He knew they were asking themselves if it was the German's threats that had already cowed the mob before he faced them or if, by chance, he possessed some extraordinary hypnotic power which he had exercised. But whichever decision they came to in their own minds he knew that from this moment the German was his deadly enemy. Ricardo had supported Cara Hume out of the saloon, and now Rushton spoke as if nothing at all had happened to upset the tranquillity of the gathering.

"I think I can supply what is missing," he said at last, looking at the others, one after the other. "But I must have time to think it over. These plans will need some studying."

"Then you'll do the studying in here and I'll sit with you," responded the German.

The answer was a blow to the plan that was forming in Rushton's mind, but he betrayed no sign.

"That suits me all right. But I can't tackle them to-night. I'll think about them and get to work early in the morning."

"We'll be off Las Palmas by then," said Mrs. Rentley.

"We'll be off Las Palmas to-night," snapped the German.

Then he gathered up the plans. "In the morning, then," he added surly.

With that he rose and went into his cabin. He came out a few minutes later and passed them without another word, making for the deck.

The two Dutchmen followed him. Mrs. Rentley turned to Rushton.

"I hope you'll be able to make good," she said quietly. "You have no friend in Muller."

Rushton shrugged and helped himself to a cigarette from a box on the table.

"Why should personal feelings enter into a thing like this?" he asked her. "We are out to do a certain job, aren't we?"

"Yes, but Muller is not pleased that I have brought you in. He is not forgetting that you were Gilson's man."

"Can't a man change jobs?" he asked curtly.

"I know and I understand because I overheard your row. But Muller is—difficult. He is not jealous. He would not confess to such weakness. But he is not pleased that I have shown an interest in you."

"Trouble usually starts when there is a woman, and a charming one, in the case," he came back quickly, for her remark had given him an opening he had been working for. "And by the same token, what about that girl who almost put everyone by the ears. It was a mistake to allow Ricardo to bring her along."

"I could not prevent him. Ricardo, you see, is one of those who holds the money-bags."

Now Rushton could understand why even Muller hadn't been discourteous to Ricardo nor chided him for his weakness.

"Well, it was a mistake. If that gang get quarrelling over the girl it will need more than Ricardo's money to keep them in hand. I wish you would take my advice."

"What is it?"

"Keep her out of sight—in a cabin where she won't come into contact with any of those precious fellows."

"You take a keen interest in her, my friend."

He professed a cold anger.

"I have an interest in just one thing," he rasped. "I want this thing to be a success. Do you think I have taken such a step without weighing the cost? It is only because of the promise of big reward. So am I going to see the whole thing blow up through a chit of a girl?"

She laughed.

"All right, I'll do what I can, but I fancy Ricardo will see to it now. By the way, just how did you manage to quell that attack that was on the verge of breaking? Muller thinks it was what he said, but I know it wasn't. There is something there that I don't understand. If I thought I had made a mistake about you—"

"It was what Muller said," he assured her. "And if you are going to start getting suspicious now—well, let us have a showdown all round."

She gave him a very straight look.

"I didn't accept you without considerable reflection. I am not easily impressed by your sex, Mr. Rushton. But you baffle me sometimes. I don't know yet whether to be glad or sorry that you were wearing a bullet-proof shirt when I tried to shoot you the first time. You may wonder that a woman should choose the life I do. I may give you my reasons one day. But I have chanced more on you than ever before upon any man. Muller can tell you that. If I have been mistaken —but I don't want to be. I believe you and I could go far together."

Rushton could not profess to misunderstand her words or the look that accompanied them. He wondered how successful his daring bluff would have gone had her personal feelings not been engaged.

He realised that this only complicated matters. As long as she felt that way towards him she would be lenient in her judgment and heaven knows he needed every asset in his present position.

On the other hand, if she began to doubt, if she felt herself rebuffed in any way, if he injured her pride, his position would become one of such peril that his life would be worthless.

"You have put me to the test," he said smoothly. "Do you think it is not the more agreeable to me that you are here? If you take the trouble to go into my past life you will find that women have played no part in it. I have lived too hard to have time for that sort of thing. But you—you are—different."

"I am glad we have had this talk," she whispered. "But we must be careful. Look out for Muller. And now I am going to give you something. Muller doesn't want you to have a gun yet. But I am going to give you one. Take it.

She pushed her own gun across to him and Rushton's fingers closed on it quickly. Next moment it was in his pocket. A great feeling of relief came over him. He had been figuring hard how to get hold of a weapon and now he had achieved his purpose without the risk of questions being asked. He felt honestly grateful to her and sorry that he must dissemble. But he was fighting too big a game to be baulked by lesser things.

She opened her bag and took out three spare loaded clips of cartridges which she passed him. Rushton dropped them into his pocket.

"I won't forget this," he assured her quietly, and he meant it. Nor was the day far distant when he was going to repay the debt, though neither of them knew that then.

"Remember what I have said and my warning," she returned. "And now I'll go and look after that girl. You see how I defer to your judgment, yet I think you may be right."

They both rose, and while she went out by the door leading to the corridor, Rushton ascended to the deck. He was bent upon a definite purpose, but he knew that every move he made would be watched.

CHAPTER X

CLAYTON FRICK was in a position of almost supreme control of affairs during the absence of Sir Charles Gilson.

The routine work of the offices was, of course, carried on as usual by the staff. But in his position as Sir Charles's confidential assistant and secretary, Frick was the mouthpiece to issue instructions left by his principal.

When he had first entered the service of the shipowner he had had no thought of betraying his trust. Not that he was worried by any ethical consideration. On the contrary, Clayton Frick was possessed with a consuming ambition to make money, lots and lots of it, and he didn't care two straws how he made it.

But, at that time, he figured he had just as good a chance of achieving his ambition by playing straight and taking advantage of any tips Sir Charles might give him as by running crooked.

And that hope had been realised. There were more than crumbs to be picked up at the shipowner's table. Sir Charles was always deep in some financial game, and, quietly, without his knowledge, Frick could take a hand more often than not.

The result had been a very substantial addition to his resources, and it is possible that he would have continued along these lines had it not been for his meeting with the Countess de Saladier, otherwise the 'Orchid.'

If it is true that every man has his price (and every woman too) then Clayton Frick had his. And when it was dangled before his eyes by such a person as the 'Orchid' it possessed a lure that made it all the more desirable.

Besides, what she offered promised in one rich coup more than he had hoped to amass over many years. Therefore, with Sir Charles's interests in direct conflict with his own, it was the shipowner's that went under.

Frick knew his job. He was efficient and painstaking. There wasn't a phase of Sir Charles's affairs that hadn't been mastered by him, with the exception of the secret plans which Sir Charles was working on regarding the floating drome that was to be moored in the South Atlantic.

Not even to Frick did Sir Charles disclose that secret. Not that he mistrusted him. He was simply not ready to share it with anyone until the right moment came.

But he didn't know that Frick had been promised fifty thousand pounds to play his pal in the desperate attempt to secure them, though he did know that whoever was the first in the field with such a landing drome would realise millions through the eventual development of such a monopoly.

He believed then that success was within his grasp when Sir Charles sailed in the *Corsair*. He knew that Rushton was going along to guard Sir Charles and the plans. He didn't know just how Sir Charles would appear on the scene but he could guess a lot and his information was passed on to the Saladiers.

Neither he nor they knew that Mrs. Rentley and Ricardo would be travelling in the same ship nor that there was opposed to the Saladiers a gang with even greater resources and composed of persons even more determined and desperate.

It can be understood, therefore, how perturbed he was when the message came telling him of the fiasco on board the *Corsair* instead of an announcement of success.

He knew that it finished him with Sir Charles. He knew that Rushton would soon ferret out his connection with the Saladiers. Therefore something must be done and quickly.

He canvassed the possibilities. No one else in the offices could possibly know what was happening. So far the secret was his, and that gave him time to act. But Sir Charles would lose no time in disposing of him as soon as he reached Las Palmas.

The thing to do was to act first, and deciding thus, Frick made up his mind to play his hand to the limit.

His first care was to realise all his assets. He had always kept them in a financially liquid form so that was easy. Next he examined the situation in connection with Sir Charles's affairs and found he could help himself to ten or twelve thousand pounds without much immediate risk. Later, discovery must come anyway, and by that time he hoped to be well clear.

Finally, he decided that he must get to Las Palmas in the shortest possible time. That meant by aeroplane.

Within twenty-four hours he was ready. At the offices he simply said that he was going away on urgent business for Sir Charles, so not the slightest suspicion was aroused.

It was a simple matter to arrange for a private aeroplane to take him. From Heston he flew by stages, to Daker, and from there it was a direct oversea hop to Las Palmas.

At seven o'clock a few days later his plane landed up near Monte from where they could look down upon Las Palmas and the wide sweep of the bay with its shipping. But the *Corsair* wasn't there. She had already made her brief call and departed.

Frick had sent no word of his coming either to Sir Charles Gilson or the Saladiers. He knew where to find both parties if they were in Las Palmas.

As soon as he had finished his arrangements at the landing ground, he secured a car at Monte and drove straight down to Las Palmas, some six miles by road.

He knew that Sir Charles would be at the Metropole, if anywhere. The Saladiers would have gone to a smaller and much quieter hotel that had been spoken of before the *Corsair* left England.

It was to this hotel, the Inglesa, that he drove and, as he hoped, found the Saladier gang, released from the *Corsair* on account of lack of evidence, installed in a series of communicating rooms on the first floor overlooking the harbour.

It was with relief that they saw him enter. At the moment, the Saladiers were very much in the air over the whole thing that had been planned with such nicety. They had anticipated trouble in dealing with Grant Rushton. They had known nothing definite about Mrs. Rentley until the ground had been cut away from beneath their feet. Of course, before reaching Las Palmas they had managed to learn something of what had happened on board, but, even now, they were considerably in the dark about details.

Frick got the whole story immediately. He heard about the various attempts that had been made to secure the plans. He was told about the murder of the Brown Priest. They still believed Rushton was responsible for that. They related how there had been a dramatic invasion and killing in Sir Charles Gilson's cabin.

Then they told Frick how Sir Charles and Rushton had quarrelled and how four persons had vanished from the ship before they reached Las Palmas. There had been no particular effort made to conceal that. It was generally known on board. They even knew the identity of the four—the man, Ricardo, Cara Hume, Mrs. Rentley and Rushton.

Frick listened moodily to the story. He made no comment until the countess, who had done the telling, had finished. Then he smiled crookedly.

"They have fooled you," he said harshly.

Her dark eyes flashed.

"What do you mean, monsieur?"

At the beginning of Frick's participation in the Saladier scheme he had been, more or less, under the orders of the Saladiers. But now, curiously enough, he seemed to be assuming the leadership. As a matter of fact his mind was far superior to that of any of the others with the possible exception of the 'Orchid.'

"I mean this," he said curtly. "That quarrel between Sir Charles Gilson and Rushton was staged to deceive the others. They would never quarrel. Rushton would never betray Sir Charles. He is too single-tracked in his mental make-up. That was a shrewd move."

"But this other crowd of whom we did not learn until too late. This Mrs. Rentley as she called herself, what about her? It is known that she left the ship and we know where she went. We received some wireless messages. They could not withhold them from us. And they could not bring any evidence against us for the shooting was done while we were under arrest."

"If Rushton went with this person who calls herself Mrs. Rentley then he is playing a deep game. He has gone after the plans. I know the man, I tell you. He will not give up until the thing is finished one way or another. You say you know where they went. Where is it?"

"There is a ship full of criminals that has been cruising about the seas for some months. We know—"

Frick interrupted her with a gesture.

"I know the ship you mean. The papers have had plenty in them about it. So that is it, is it? That is bad, very bad. You say there was a man called Ricardo. I know what crowd they are now. There are South American interests who have been after those plans. They approached me tentatively, but I had already gone in with you. There is plenty of money behind that gang. This wants some thinking out. Did Sir Charles land here?"

"Yes. We have had him under observation constantly. There is a flying boat in the harbour. He is going to use that for some purpose."

"That means he is going to fly from here to where the drome will be anchored."

"But will he leave without his plans? And his two men have been killed."

"He may count on Rushton regaining possession of them. Let me think."

He lighted a cigarette and paced the room. He was asking himself if the other gang had secured possession of everything. He knew more about the plans than Sir Charles Gilson had believed. He was perfectly aware that Sir Charles had taken particular care of a vital, key part.

Where was that? Was it gone? Or did Sir Charles still have possession of it? The rest of the plans were useless without it and, *per contra,* that vital part could not be applied without the other portions.

Sir Charles—he was the key to the thing as it stood—he and Rushton. For Frick did not believe for a single moment that the row which had taken place on board was anything more than a cooked-up bluff between Sir Charles and Rushton. He knew better than the others what sort of man Grant Rushton was. He told himself, without any sense of personal shame from the implied comparison, that Rushton would never sell out Sir Charles.

He turned quickly to the countess. He gave her his conclusions. She agreed with him. It was she and Frick now who were handling things. The others were mere cyphers.

"And what do you propose, monsieur?" she asked, eyeing him with a new interest.

"The fact that I have cut things in England and come on here is sufficient proof that I am chancing everything on this affair, isn't it?"

"I am perfectly willing to grant that."

"We've got to secure those plans now. Everything hangs on it. The question is—how far are we prepared to go?"

"I can answer for myself, my companions and my principals," she said evenly. "We go to what you call it—the limit."

"Good. So do I. Now let us plan the first step. As I see it, Sir Charles is the key of the thing at the moment. Therefore we must get possession of that key."

"You mean—actually?"

"I mean just what I say."

"And then, monsieur?"

"We would hold a strong card. But we cannot advance past that point until we come to some arrangement with the other people."

"You mean make them a proposal?"

"Exactly. We can reach that ship by wireless, can't we?"

"Of course."

"They will have to deal with us. We shall offer to join them and split the profits."

"And if they refuse?"

"They can't. I tell you Sir Charles with that key part of the plans or his knowledge which can produce it again if it has been destroyed puts us in a position to dictate."

"But to share—" she began.

Frick grinned at her.

"Let us play each hand as it is dealt," he said. "We can settle that point later. The thing is to make contact quickly. If they agree we can arrange about a motor boat here soon enough. We could join them out at sea."

Her eyes rested on him admiringly.

"I understand now, monsieur. It is a pleasure to listen to you. And it is fortunate that you have come. You and I—we can do this thing." And she shot a veiled look of contempt at her husband.

"Very well. Send one of your crowd off at once to see about a motor boat, a good sea boat. Agree to any terms. It won't be coming back anyway."

"And you?"

"I'm going to call upon Sir Charles Gilson in two hours. That should give plenty of time to fix things. Let us compose a message to the people in the *Santa Cruz*"

He lit a cigarette and looked at her with a curious glance.

"Rushton, eh? I'll fix Rushton before this thing is finished."

CHAPTER XI

SIR CHARLES GILSON had no option but to leave the *Corsair* at Las Palmas.

It was perfectly useless for him to continue on to the spot in the South Atlantic where the floating drome was to be anchored until he had recovered the plans.

Were Green and Follet still alive it would have been possible to set them to work under his personal direction and get out another set of the general designs.

But, to attempt it alone, would mean a very long job. He would need many weeks, possibly months even allowing for his knowledge of the original draughting to assist him.

He was forced, therefore, into a period of inaction while waiting to learn what Rushton could accomplish. He did not blame Rushton in the least for what had happened on board the *Corsair*. It would have been far beyond the powers of any one man to cope with what had arisen.

It had been a mistake to travel in the *Corsair*. Although the tragic occurrences had not touched the passengers closely it had been impossible to smother them entirely. It would be a bad thing if the *Corsair* received a black eye on her first voyage.

But things on board were all right now. The whole thing was like a bad dream to Sir Charles. He rubbed his plastered head thoughtfully as he sat in his private sitting-room pondering on matters.

Rushton was taking an awful risk. But he had insisted. It was the only thing to be done. If he failed it would mean certain death. If he succeeded against such overwhelming odds—well he would have earned a big reward.

Rushton had cast certain reflections upon Frick. There, Sir Charles did not see quite eye to eye with him. Frick may have been indiscreet but surely not treacherous. He had always seemed so quiet and efficient and dependable.

The idea of chartering a private plane and returning to England entered his head. He considered, too, the plan of reporting the affair to the British Government and asking their aid. After all, that floating drome in the South Atlantic would mean a big asset to all the British Mercantile Marine.

He could fly to England by way of Lisbon. He could spend a couple of days in England and then return if necessary. The more he considered the idea the more he favoured it. And, while there, he could make arrangements about a new set of plans as well as to examine Frick.

He had just reached this conclusion when there came a knock at the door. He called a permission to enter. The door opened and, to his astonishment, Frick appeared.

"Good heavens, Frick, what are you doing out here and how did you get here?" he demanded.

"I took it upon myself to come, sir," said Frick smiling easily.

"But why?"

"You have been injured, sir. I hope it is not serious."

"Oh, this." Sir Charles indicated his head. "No, it is not much. But how did you know?"

"I will explain, sir. Certain matters have come up in London about which it was necessary to consult you personally. I tried to get in touch with you on board the *Corsair* by wireless. I received a reply from the captain informing me that you had met with an accident and had left the ship at Las Palmas. I debated what to do. Then it occurred to me that I could reach Las Palmas by air and explain matters to you in person. I reached Monte this morning."

"Well, I must say you acted with decision, Frick. What has happened?"

"Well, sir, I learned one or two things in London that made me uneasy about you and the purpose of your journey. I received anonymous communications warning me that you were in danger. I do not know who could have sent them. But when I heard about your accident I became more anxious. Therefore I decided to come."

Sir Charles regarded him in silence. He appeared very serious and earnest. His manner certainly did not suggest that he had been up to any treachery. In fact his solicitude was rather touching. Surely Rushton couldn't be right.

"And what happened in London, Frick?"

Frick hesitated and glanced about him.

"I've got some papers to show you, sir. I don't quite understand them but I think they refer to the floating drome. I believe you ought to see them. I brought them with me but have left them in my document case in the plane by which I travelled. You see, I did not know if I should be in time to find you here. I did not know what fresh plans you might have made."

"Well, now that you have found me you'd better get them, hadn't you? I'd like to go into them at once."

"It would save time, sir, if you drove up to Monte with me. I have a car at the door and, if you will permit me to say so, Sir Charles, a drive up to that height would do you good."

"All right, I don't mind. Wait until I put some cigars in my case."

He was soon ready. They descended to the ground floor and went out to the street, where a hired saloon car was waiting. Frick helped Sir Charles in and spoke to the driver, an island Spaniard.

He got in beside Sir Charles and the car moved off. They began to go down towards the old part of the town rather than in the direction that Sir Charles expected, and he turned to Frick with a frown.

"Is this the way? It isn't as I remember it."

"He is taking a roundabout way to pick up the new road, sir. He is going the same route by which he brought me down."

Sir Charles grunted and looked out of the windows. They had turned into a narrow cobbled street lined with small, mean houses such as form the old part of Las Palmas.

Sir Charles was thinking that, if it was necessary to go this way in order to pick up the new road in order to make the short run to Monte, it would have been better to take the old route.

Then suddenly, he remembered what Grant Rushton had said. A quick feeling of uneasiness assailed him. He took the cigar out of his mouth and turned to Frick.

"This is nonsense, Frick," he exploded. "I don't like this at all."

"And you won't like this either," were the last words of which he was conscious as Frick, turning on him with an evil smile that revealed things all too late, slammed a soaking pad across his mouth and held him while his struggles grew more and more feeble and finally ceased.

The car continued on its way. Frick eased the unconscious man back so that he was reclining in the corner in a way that would appear natural enough to any casual observer. But Frick wasn't worrying about curious eyes in that part of the town.

They turned deeper into the old part and then came out near the edge of the harbour, but some distance now from where the wharves and jetties of the big shipping firms were located.

Then they were among some trees, and emerging from these,

came into a road that curved round towards a dilapidated jetty. At the end of this a large, cabined motor boat was moored.

The car drove right on to the jetty and stopped. As it did so, the two gunmen of the Saladier gang appeared and scrambled on to the jetty. One of them opened the door. Frick grinned at him and hauled the unconscious Sir Charles towards him and pushed him into the waiting arms of the other two. They carried him across the jetty and over the side of the boat. Frick got out and passed the driver a roll of money. The fellow grinned and at once began to back the car off the jetty. Frick jumped aboard. He was met by the countess, who gave him a smile of congratulation.

They disappeared into the cabin where some flimsies of wireless messages lay on the table.

"What is the decision?" asked Frick briskly.

"They have accepted the proposition, monsieur. They agree to participate on the terms we offered. They will wait for us fifteen miles out at sea. So you were right. Our unconscious guest is the key to the puzzle."

"Did you put them on their guard about Rushton?"

"No. I thought it better to wait until we got there. We do not know how conditions are on board. We shall have to go very carefully. Once we join them we cannot retreat."

"We'll hold our own with that mob," he returned confidently. "We'd better get away at once. If that driver splits there'll be a hue and cry in no time."

Within five minutes the motor boat was speeding across the harbour towards the open sea.

CHAPTER XII

IT was night, and Herman Muller was alone in his cabin on board the *Santa Cruz*.

He was in the devil's own temper. One might have thought that he would find some cause for satisfaction in the fact that Mrs. Rentley had carried out her work on board the *Corsair* with a swift and deadly efficiency that would meet with even his icy approval.

So it would ordinarily. But he had not counted on her appearing in company with the man who had been the greatest obstacle in their way. For he did not share her confidence in Grant Rushton.

Muller was a better judge of men than Mrs. Rentley. One glance at Rushton's steady eyes and lean jaw, his complete coolness under what could only be regarded as a risky situation, were enough to convince Muller that Rushton was not the man to sell out his own interests.

This unwilling tribute to Rushton's sense of honour did not soften his opinion. On the contrary, it only increased his distrust.

Moreover, he was none too pleased at Mrs. Rentley's manner towards him. Muller was no weakling in regard to women. He looked upon them as of an entirely different species from men, and, in moments of relaxation, to be treated as toys.

His attitude towards Mrs. Rentley was not quite that. In her he saw something rather superior to the usual run of her sex and he had to confess that she was more valuable in some situations than most men he had worked with.

But he had only one mind when it came to business. He never would have consented to her being in the thing at all but he had been overruled by the financial powers who controlled the affair, and, in view of her capability, he had grudgingly confessed to himself that she would do.

But her arrival with Rushton, her way of looking at him, her insistence that he was playing straight when he had thrown in his lot with them, filled Muller with deep anger. Rushton may have fooled her, he might fool the others but he couldn't fool Muller.

Nor did Ricardo's exploits lessen his temper.

His arrival with a girl in whom he showed a jealous possession was another sore point.

What was the thing becoming? he asked himself. Were they engaged upon a serious business, a matter that involved millions, or were they running a honeymoon cruise?

A nice mixture, he rumbled to himself as he pawed the plans that Mrs. Rentley had brought. A ship full of several hundred criminals who couldn't produce one among them who didn't count murder as one of his crimes, sentimental sex stuff mixed in with that, and the vital part of the plans still missing. To be dependent upon the new recruit, Rushton, for that missing part didn't appeal to Muller. The fellow had all sorts of chances to fake the thing.

He had just decided that he would have a private talk with the two Dutchmen, the van Korsens, when there came a double knock at the door.

Muller glanced quickly at his watch. It was just after midnight. Perhaps he was wanted on the bridge. The navigation staff, at least, could be depended upon.

He stepped across and turned back the key, jerking the door open as he did so.

His astonishment on seeing Grant Rushton on the threshold was punctuated by the muzzle of a pistol in his stomach.

"Step back, Muller," ordered Rushton, keeping his tone low.

Muller could do nothing but obey. His own gun was on the table that was screwed to the floor under the porthole.

Rushton half-circled, forcing Muller to move contra wise. Thus he worked his way over so that he could reach out and get hold of Muller's gun. He caught it in his left hand and then dropped it in his pocket. But he did not lower his own weapon. Muller might have another gun in his pocket.

Rushton had seen something else. He had seen the plans lying where Muller had been studying them. Still threatening Muller, Rushton managed to get his hands on them and drop them in his coat pocket.

Muller hadn't uttered a sound. He had obeyed every order, but his eyes were coldly furious, and Rushton knew well enough that he would seize the first opening.

"That's that, Muller," he said quietly. "I think you knew I'd get hold of these things at the first opportunity, so I didn't waste any time."

"Much good it will do you," snarled Muller, and Rushton noticed that he didn't attempt to raise his voice. He realised well enough that Rushton would jerk back on the trigger on the instant. "If you expect to get away with them you are mad. Or will you hand them to Mrs. Rentley to take care of?"

"I'll manage all right," Rushton assured him coolly. "You see—"

He never finished the sentence. At that moment, the ship heaved upwards as if caught by a sudden squall. It wasn't a very severe roll but served to send Rushton swaying backwards so that the gun jerked away from Muller's ribs.

And, quick as lightning to seize the chance, Muller struck Rushton's arm a hard, sideways blow, then drove his foot straight at Rushton's body.

Rushton pulled the trigger at Muller's first movement. But the bullet ripped along the side of Muller's coat and thudded into the wall behind him.

The kick almost doubled Rushton up in a sudden sharp pain. Muller had hold of his arm but if he wanted to fight with all the rules off Rushton was willing. There were no rules in this game anyway.

He threw up his left arm and held Muller with a fist drive. Then he jerked the barrel of the pistol round and fired again. There was no mistake this time. Muller went down. The bullet had gone through his heart.

Rushton made for the door. There were too many ears on board that ship for the sound of the shots to pass unheeded. He closed the door softly and started through the saloon.

Footsteps came rattling down the companion that led to the deck. Rushton reached the door that led to the corridor by which he could reach the old music saloon.

He jerked it open and leaped through, closing it after him. Then he sprinted down the corridor. But, in the distance, he saw his way blocked by a bulky figure. It was Ricardo.

Rushton lifted his gun to fire, but Ricardo, sensing his danger, dived into a cabin. Rushton kept on and reached a secondary companion by which he could reach the deck. It was mostly used by the engine-room staff.

He was half way up when he heard Ricardo yelling in the corridor. Other voices took up the cry. Rushton gained the deck and sprinted forward, weaving his way among the drunken, gambling groups of criminals.

Behind him the pursuit was in full cry. The Dutchmen had joined Ricardo. He didn't know what others there would be but he knew the bridge crowd would be dangerous.

He dived into the passage that went under the bridge deck. It connected the waist with the forward part.

He emerged among a thick pack of the criminals. This was their real hangout.

After leaving the meeting in the saloon he had done a good deal of prowling about the decks. He had been looking for something and he had found it. He had not made that venture into Muller's cabin without seeing to his retreat.

But he had not counted on being pressed so hotly. It was Muller's fault for precipitating matters. He heard more shouts, and then several of the criminals seemed to join the chase, for there arose a terrific uproar behind him.

Rushton kept on. He was through the mob of criminals here before they seemed to realise what was happening. Then he made a leap for an iron ladder and gained the forecastle head.

Men were climbing after him. They reached the higher level, then one of them gave a shout and pointed. Where they had seen the fugitive a moment before there was now no one. But, curving towards the water was a human figure.

Men rushed to the side and watched while it was swept astern. Ricardo and the two Dutchmen came up. Two men from the bridge guard were on their heels.

Next moment they were racing back. Someone on the bridge signalled the engine-room. The ship came round and the searchlight sprang out to sweep over the water.

Back and forth and round and round the *Santa Cruz* steamed, but not a sign of the fugitive could be seen. One solitary thing rewarded them. It was one of the ship's lifebuoys. But Rushton wasn't clinging to it. He was gone.

CHAPTER XIII

NEXT morning when a meeting was held in the saloon the atmosphere was sultry.

The gathering was much smaller than on the preceding day. There was Mrs. Rentley looking pale, and, for once, decidedly discomposed.

The two van Korsens were sitting beside each other as usual. They never were very talkative but on this occasion they were almost dumb. It was they who had first come running at the sound of the shots and had found Muller's dead body.

Of course, Ricardo was present and now he sat in Muller's chair at the head of the table. Mrs. Rentley was opposite him. Grant Rushton was absent.

The subjects under discussion were the killing of Muller, the disappearance of the plans, and the vanishing of Rushton—three very unpleasant subjects to have on the agenda.

The elder Dutch brother, Jan van Korsen, had made one of his rare speeches. He had asked if, now that the plans were gone and Muller was dead, the affair would be abandoned. It was here that Ricardo showed himself as being more of a factor than they had considered.

"Why should we abandon it?" he demanded hotly. "Who are you to make such a proposal? Muller is gone; well that's unfortunate, but it doesn't mean that we are going to close down. What do you think I am doing here? Where does the money come from? Don't you get it into your heads that, because I have been willing to see Muller direct things I haven't been watching things. Of course we go ahead, and you can look to me for orders."

Mrs. Rentley nodded vigorously.

"Ricardo is right. We cannot throw in our hand now. Why should we?"

Hugo van Korsen stirred his thick body. "What do you propose? The plans are gone aren't they? And your friend," he sneered at Mrs. Rentley, "is gone with them. This would never have happened if you hadn't brought him on board. He fooled you up to the hilt. Muller was right—serious business is no place for a woman. They are ruled by their emotions. It was a crazy thing to do."

Mrs. Rentley bit her lip. She would have liked to have been able to answer such taunts in a way that would have stopped them very quickly. But now, what could she say? Every word was true. Rushton had fooled her. She had been as easy as a child. And she knew, in her heart of hearts, that it had been easy for him because he had appealed to her in his own person.

"I made a mistake," she said at last, coldly, "let it go at that. But you will not forget that it was I who secured those plans against great odds."

Ricardo, who wasn't anxious to have his own weakness regarding Cara Hume brought up, nodded in quick agreement with her.

"Quarrelling and reproaches will do no good," he said. "We must work together, and there is no time to lose. Let us lay things out and consider them. We know that Rushton went to Muller's cabin last night and shot him."

The van Korsens nodded together.

"Right then," went on Ricardo, "he killed Muller and took the plans. Then he dived overboard. Now, what became of him after that? We searched the whole area within a two miles radius of the ship. There wasn't a sign of him. We found a lifebuoy that belongs to this ship. How did it get in the water? Did Rushton grab it and pitch it over before he went himself? Or was it thrown by someone else? If so, then it means that he has a confederate on board.

The van Korsens looked towards Mrs. Rentley. She went still paler with renewed anger.

"Don't look at me that way," she snapped. "I knew nothing about it. I was undressed and in my bunk. Ricardo can tell you. He saw me in a dressing-gown when I came out to see what had happened."

"Yes, that is so," Ricardo confirmed.

"What about that girl?" asked Hugo van Korsen. "Could she have done it?"

"Impossible," said Mrs. Rentley. "She was in her berth. I had seen her there a few minutes before. It is my opinion that Rushton threw the lifebuoy over or took it with him when he jumped. He lost his hold and could not recover it or failed to reach it. He took a desperate chance and lost. He may have been swept in under the propellers and killed, or he may have sunk at once. At any rate, he is gone, and I believe the plans are gone with him."

"He could not swim the distance to land," added Ricardo. "The nearest point is forty miles distant. I agree with Mrs. Rentley. I think he is finished."

"Then what are we to do if the plans are gone too?" asked Jan van Korsen glumly. "If no plans exist we cannot gain possession of them. And the only person who can make new ones is Sir Charles Gilson. It is a pity Mrs. Rentley didn't bring him aboard instead of the other."

"He is in Las Palmas," said Ricardo slowly.

They all looked at him. The same idea struck them all. Ricardo nodded.

"You have guessed my meaning. Isn't that the solution? And I may say that I have—friends in Las Palmas."

"The Saladiers may have seen the same idea," put in Mrs. Rentley.

Before Ricardo could answer the door of the saloon opened, and the bearded man and buck negro who had intruded the night before, lounged in. They leant up against the wall and surveyed the group at the table. It was the bearded one who spoke.

"What's it all about?" he drawled. "Are you discussing what I said last night? The boys want action, not promises. Or is it what *happened* last night?"

Ricardo frowned.

"You will know in good time, Keeler. How can we make our plans with you fellows walking in and interrupting us at any time you choose?"

He hadn't the compelling eye that Muller had possessed.

"Well, boss," drawled Keeler, "you can't do anything without us, and the boys have elected me permanent spokesman. We've decided we want to know what's going to be done. And what about last night? Where's Fritz?" In such familiar terms did he refer to the dead German.

"You know that Muller was shot by the fellow who came aboard," Ricardo growled in exasperation.

Keeler showed yellow teeth in a grin.

"Well, what became of him?" he persisted.

"Everyone in the ship knows he went over the side," answered Ricardo more quietly, for Mrs. Rentley had shot him a warning glance.

"Is anything changed by that? Did he get away with anything that mattered? You'd better remember, mister, that you can only go as far as we say, so you'd better let us in on what's doing."

"Haven't we made a deal with you?" demanded Ricardo. "Haven't you been promised your share in the cash-out?"

"Promised, yes. Well, I won't press you, but I warn you we want to see something happen soon. The boys want to get this job finished and then land somewhere. If you can't deal with your own gang, turn the trouble-maker over to us. We'll tame him—or her—all right." And with that he grinned evilly at Mrs. Rentley.

Just how the situation might have developed is doubtful, but it didn't come to a crisis then for the door burst open and one of the bridge men came in. He was one of Ricardo's navigators hired at a fixed wage with no promised share in the venture upon which they were bound.

He handed Ricardo a sheet of paper.

"Wireless message just come in from Las Palmas," he announced. "Any answer, sir?"

Those at the table bent closer. They forgot, for the moment, that Keeler and the negro were listening with all ears.

Ricardo read the message, first to himself and then aloud.

"Listen to this," he said. "It is from the Saladiers, if you please. It says: 'Are fully informed your position regarding vital part of plans. Are in position to produce person vital to this difficulty. Are you prepared make deal with us to join you on equal sharing basis? Answer immediately as quick action essential. Saladier, Hotel Inglesa, Las Palmas.'"

"It means," said Mrs. Rentley, "it means just what I said. They can get hold of Gilson."

"Well, what'll we do?"

Ricardo looked at the van Korsens.

"What do you say, Jan? And you, Hugo?"

"It's a good suggestion," responded the elder Dutchman after a glance at his brother. "If they can do as they say, that is."

"That's up to them. But I don't like the idea of splitting with them. We've got to pay out enough as it is."

"We can always find a way out of that," said Mrs. Rentley softly.

Ricardo nodded.

"That's right. Well, let's get an answer away. Give me a piece of paper, Jan. I'll write something." He wrote busily for a few moments, then he looked up. "How does this sound? 'We are willing to come to arrangement if you can produce goods. Reply just what you propose and how to make contact.' "

They agreed that this would do, so the message was despatched. No one knew just when Keeler and the negro had departed. They had been too engrossed. And, likewise, no one had asked what had become of the man whom Rushton had knocked against the side of the saloon the night before.

Two more messages were sent and received between them and the Saladiers during the morning. This interchange took place just before Frick went to call upon Sir Charles Gilson at the Metropole Hotel. But by that time a rendezvous had been fixed and both gangs of precious crooks were already planning to double-cross each other. They did not consider there was any other serious factor to contend with. They might have thought differently had they known where Keeler betook himself when he left the saloon.

His course led him along among the drinking, gambling groups on deck. In the glare of the sunny morning the ship was a deplorable sight. The decks had not been washed since the cargo of criminals left South America except what sluicing the rain had given them. Dirt and confusion were everywhere. The human element presented an appalling sight in such a light. Ricardo might have paused to ask himself what would happen if they really took it into their heads to assume complete control of the ship instead of exhibiting only a contemptuous tolerance of those who liked to think they were masters.

But it was all usual enough to Keeler. He had no eye for the filthy surroundings through which he swaggered. When one drunken fellow reeled into his way he gave him a backhander that sent him into the scuppers. He didn't even look to see if the fellow would attempt to draw a knife on him.

Then he dived into the forecastle, which was so dimly lit that it was almost impossible to see one's way between the bunks. But that didn't bother Keeler. He kept right on to the end and bent down over the very last bunk.

"Are you awake?" he asked in a voice that would have amazed Ricardo, so full of respect was it.

Out of the gloom came a reply.

"That you, Keeler? Yes. What is it? Any news?"

"Plenty. They're in touch with someone in Las Palmas. Listen: this is what I heard."

He told into the darkness what had passed in the saloon. The invisible one listened in silence. Then he gave vent to a smothered oath.

"You've done a bit of good work, Keeler. Can you carry on?"

"Sure, I can carry on. I know you'll do what you say. As long as I know that I can handle this bunch of scum."

"What about the girl, Keeler?"

"Saw and heard nothing."

"Keep me posted, then. I know what that Las Palmas business means. There's going to be hell popping in this ship before the finish, Keeler. Make sure of your end of it. I think you'll find that they are making a deal with those people in Las Palmas. Find out if they are coming aboard. This is urgent. And, later, I want you to get a note into the hand of that girl. Understand?"

"I can do that."

"And keep your scum away from her. Get me?"

"It isn't the men as much as that fellow Ricardo."

"I'll put him where I put Muller. Now get me some food and a drink, will you?"

"Sure I will, boss."

Keeler left the forecastle on his errand. Down in the saloon the gang were still debating the Saladier message and waiting for a reply to the message they had sent.

Grant Rushton lit a cigarette and sat up in the gloom of the forecastle. He was thinking just then how neatly Keeler had dumped over the side the dead body of the dwarf whose neck Rushton had broken, thus making the gang-leaders think that Rushton was drowned.

He ground out the end of the cigarette as he saw Keeler's bulk silhouetted against the oblong of the doorway.

CHAPTER XIV

IT wasn't as coincidental as it might seem that Grant Rushton should have recognised Keeler as a man he had come into contact with in South America.

The whole six hundred and more criminals on board the *Santa Cruz* had been cleared out of their haunts in one country in that continent. Two years before, Rushton had spent six months on a dangerous job that took him through the underworld of Rio Janeiro and Buenos Aires. He had met Keeler in a particularly tough dive on the waterfront of Rio.

There was no sentiment in the rough friendship that had been born between them on that occasion. Keeler was one of the worst characters among the scum of Rio. Rushton had made use of him in pursuing his own ends. Keeler had simply sold his services for money, and Rushton had paid well. That was all.

But it was sufficient to give a fresh twist to Rushton's plans when he recognised Keeler on board the hell-ship.

When the meeting in the saloon broke up he had made his way to the main deck. It had not taken him long to locate Keeler among the drinking groups. A touch on the arm and a jerk of the head were sufficient to bring Keeler trailing forward where they could talk unobserved.

Within a few minutes Rushton knew the terms upon which the ship load of criminals had agreed to throw in their lot with Muller and his gang.

Ten pounds cash to every man, with twenty-five pounds to six who bossed their own following, fifty pounds to Jonas, the nigger who had been in the cabin with Keeler, and a hundred pounds to Keeler as the big shot of the whole outfit. He was the big shot simply because he had made himself so since the hell-ship had sailed from South America.

Rushton knew he must fight with the same weapons. He knew how far he could pledge Sir Charles Gilson. Fifteen or twenty thousand pounds were a drop compared to what was at stake.

He made his deal with Keeler then and there.

"I'll double the figure for the men," he told him. "Twenty pounds for every manjack on board, fifty pounds for the petty bosses, a hundred for the nigger and you, Keeler, you'll touch five hundred of the best if you sit in with me."

"So it's as Muller suspects," said Keeler.

"Muller won't be able to suspect anything when I finish with him," growled Rushton. "You know me, Keeler. You know I'll keep my word. Do you play my hand or not?"

"Maybe the others would meet your figure?" said Keeler slyly.

"And maybe not. Don't try that, Keeler. You know I'm making you a good offer. And, at the finish, the ship is yours. You can beach her wherever you fancy. What happened in Rio is neither here nor there. But you know whether I kept my word then or not."

"I'm with you, boss. I know you and I don't know Muller. What do you want me to do?"

Rushton gave him a lead. They confabbed together for a long time. Then they parted, Rushton preparing for his visit to Muller, Keeler slinking off to sound Jonas, the nigger, and to attend to certain arrangements which Rushton had suggested.

It was as a result of this palaver that Rushton was able to vanish during the hot pursuit after the killing of Muller. The thing was handled so quickly and there was so much confusion all about that not the breath of a suspicion was roused. Only Jonas the nigger knew in addition that it was not Rushton who went over the side but the dead body of the gorilla-like fellow whom Rushton had struck in the saloon.

Not even Muller would have dared penetrate into the sinister gloom of the forecastle. That bunch of criminals were very jealous of their 'rights.'

And Keeler and Jonas, the nigger, were already busy with their whisperings and nudges and suggestions. Not a whisper of the truth leaked through to the afterguard.

But Rushton dared not come out except when he knew the coast was clear. He knew what Cara Hume would be thinking. He knew that, even though she held him in contempt for his treachery to Sir Charles, she would still feel some shreds of hope while he was on board. She would remember what had happened in the saloon.

But now she would believe he had deserted in a fresh attack of cowardly treachery. She would be utterly alone. Mrs. Rentley would give her no protection. Ricardo might do his best to protect her from the criminal scum, but even then what was her fate to be? A short spell with Ricardo himself, and after that to be cast inside some unspeakable den in South America? Cara Hume knew well enough the common fate of girls who were once trapped in that net. Little wonder that she was overcome with terror and despair.

Since the affair in the saloon she had kept to her own cabin. She was too terrified to exercise even in the corridor. It was there that the gorilla-like creature had attacked her.

Ricardo was too occupied for the moment to worry her, but even Mrs. Rentley had failed to persuade her to come out. And even her efforts had been purely perfunctory. She was too bewildered and too bitter over Rushton's defection to give any time to the girl. Indeed, had Rushton been within reach he would have found that her gun was just as quick and her aim quite as certain as she had proved them on board the *Corsair*.

It may be understood, then, that in the flimsy seclusion of her own cabin the girl was sunk in misery. In no direction could she see the slightest hope.

She did not know the full strength of what had happened, but she did know that Rushton had killed Muller, had secured the plans and had gone over the side. Mrs. Rentley had said, too, with vicious satisfaction, that he had certainly gone to his death because it was beyond any chance that he had escaped the search even if it had been possible for any human being, fully clothed, to swim forty odd miles to the nearest land.

It was very hot. Her cabin was on the starboard side and the afternoon sun was pouring in, making the small place insufferably uncomfortable.

With her door locked she was lying on the bunk trying to sleep. Her head was splitting. Her eyes burned like live coals. The tears had dried on her cheeks. She was not the sort of girl to give way easily to tears, but her courage could not stand up under the snapping of her last hope.

A sound caused her to lie perfectly still. She scarcely breathed. She thought it was someone at the door and she sat up quietly. The sound reached her again, but this time it came from another direction.

She turned her head and a scream of terror rose in her throat as she saw a great hairy arm and then the evil, bearded countenance of one of the criminals grinning at her.

She did not realise at first that it would have been impossible for him to squeeze through the porthole to reach her. And she did not grasp, either, that he was making urgent signs for her not to make a noise.

She stared at him in wide-eyed horror. She had seen him several times before. She remembered now that he had been in the saloon when she had rushed in. What did he want? Why was he making those signs?

Then she saw his hand go up, glimpsed a bit of paper between the filthy fingers. Still grinning, he flipped it through the porthole so that it fell at her feet. And with a further sign of warning he vanished up the side as he had come.

Still fearful, she bent and picked up the paper. Untwisting it she read the few words that had been scribbled upon it.

"Don't lose your courage. I'm still on board, but on your life don't let anyone know. Keep to your cabin as much as possible. It won't be long now. G.R."

She read the message again and again. Was it a hoax? Was it some devilry of Mrs. Rentley's or Ricardo's? How could it have come from Grant Rushton if he had gone over the side?

Then she remembered that his subsequent fate was wrapt in mystery. Had he never gone over the side? Was this note genuine? Was he still on board and, thrilling hope, was he not a treacherous renegade after all?

Her excited thoughts were interrupted by a sharp knocking at the door. Up to now she had been allowed to retain the key and had kept the door locked constantly.

She hastily thrust Rushton's note inside her dress and went close to the door.

"Who is it?" she asked in a low tone.

"Open the door, girl," came back Mrs. Rentley's voice.

Cara Hume turned the key. Ever since the events on board the *Corsair* all pretence had been dropped by the older woman. Had the matter been left entirely to her she would have left Cara Hume behind. She had nothing against her. She had employed her only as a blind to lend colour to the pose she had adopted, and when that was finished she had no further use for the girl's services. But she had allowed Ricardo to have his way. After all, if he wanted to burden himself with the girl that was his affair.

She had promised Grant Rushton that she would give an eye to her. That was before the death of Muller, when she would have done a lot for him.

Cara Hume's own intuition had told her that Mrs. Rentley had felt a strong personal attraction to Rushton. She knew that explained why she had received him as an ally and had faced the suspicions of Muller and the others. But since Rushton's sensational showdown things were very much altered.

Mrs. Rentley came into the cabin with a look in her eye that had been there when she was carrying out her plans so ruthlessly on board the *Corsair*. She pushed the girl towards the bunk and closed the door.

"I want to talk to you," she snapped, "and I warn you not to play any tricks. What do you know about Rushton?"

The girl gazed at her wide-eyed. She was remembering the warning Rushton had put in his note. She knew she must conceal his secret at all costs.

"About Rushton—nothing," she said in a surprised tone. "Why do you ask me?"

"Because I'm not satisfied that you're such an innocent miss as you make out."

"But I haven't seen him. I don't know anything about him. How should I, shut up in this cabin all the time."

The other woman studied her under lowered lids.

"You spoke with him in the small saloon," she said slowly.

"I told him what contempt I held him in, if that is what you mean."

"I overheard the words that passed between you, but I'm not so sure that there wasn't something else. I'm not to be trifled with, my girl. It wasn't my wish that you came along. But, now that you are here, I warn you that if I find you trying any treachery I'll kill you just as I have others."

Cara Hume was swept with a quick fear. She knew now that Mrs. Rentley was making no idle boast. She knew about the Brown Priest and about Sir Charles Gilson's two experts, knew by what a narrow margin Sir Charles himself had escaped death.

"I don't want to remain here," she said steadily. "I shall be only too glad to leave. Let me go, Mrs. Rentley. Put me in a boat and set me adrift. I'll take my chance. And I promise you I'll say nothing to a soul about things. You are a woman. Surely you can feel a little for me."

But there was nothing soft or feminine about Mrs. Rentley unless her own passions were engaged.

"Don't be a fool," she snapped. "Ricardo will dispose of you. And he wants you to come up on deck for some exercise. Come along."

Cara Hume shrank back.

"No, oh no," she protested, "please don't force me to do that."

The other caught her by the arm.

"Do as I say," she hissed. "I haven't any time to waste on you and your fancies. You can go on the bridge. No one will harm you. Depend upon Ricardo for that." She smiled maliciously. "He will take precious good care that no one touches you. Come, do as I say or I shall have you carried up. You are to take an hour each day. We've got some visitors coming aboard later, so come on."

Cara Hume could do nothing but obey. She caught up a scarf and followed Mrs. Rentley into the gangway. They went up by the 'midships companion by which Rushton had escaped, and, then, as she saw the groups of drinking, gambling criminals lounging or squatting about the waist, she shuddered.

Nor did their evil leers make matters any better. She was glad enough now to keep close to Mrs. Rentley, who moved among them as coolly and indifferently as if they didn't exist. They seemed to recognise in her one that would shoot to kill on the slightest signs of provocation. They hadn't reached the state yet when they were prepared to put the matter to the test, although she was certainly attractive enough to bring many a calculating eye upon her.

Up on the bridge, Cara Hume found Ricardo and the hired navigating officers, two men whom she had not seen before. They looked hard and tough, and they were. Muller had picked them up in Bordeaux.

In the comparative security of the bridge she could look down upon the deck packed with criminals. As she saw their numbers, their total indifference to the slightest form of discipline and their constant journeys to the rum hogshead, she realised for the first time into what a hell gang she had been thrust.

Yet, with all the drinking and gambling, she seemed to sense an air of unrest among them, and even Mrs. Rentley and the navigating officers had a look of uneasiness in their eyes. There was something stewing underneath that Cara Hume could not grasp, but the atmosphere was so charged that it presaged an eruption of some nature.

Then, as she avoided the evil upward glances of those who had discovered her on the bridge, she suddenly found herself looking straight into the eyes of the bearded ruffian who had tossed the note into her cabin.

But he was not grinning at her now. He was watching her with a threat in his eye as if he mistrusted her nearness to Mrs. Rentley.

Cara Hume shivered despite the tropic heat, then looked away. But among that scum she saw no sign of the one she sought. She began to tell herself that the note was only some form of devilry on the part of Ricardo.

CHAPTER XV

AT four o'clock in the afternoon the snow-clad peak of Teneriffe was clearly visible far away to the south-west.

Shortly after that, a speck appeared upon the water. One of the navigating officers drew Mrs. Rentley's attention to it. She caught up a pair of glasses and studied it for a few moments. Then she caught Cara Hume by the arm.

"Come, it's time for you to go back to your cabin."

The girl did not resist. Locked again in her cabin, she stood gazing out of the porthole. At first she could not see any signs of the object that had caused excitement on the bridge, but presently she made it out and knew it for a small boat approaching the ship.

She could hear signs of fresh commotion above her. Then came running footsteps in the gangway outside as someone rushed past her door. Next she heard voices and recognised those of Mrs. Rentley and Ricardo. They were cut off sharply as a door slammed.

She continued to watch the oncoming boat until she could see it distinctly as a cabin motor boat, but she could not distinguish clearly the features of the two persons who stood in the after-cockpit.

Then the craft altered its course as if to come round the stern of the *Santa Cruz*. There was a change in the rhythm of the engines. The *Santa Cruz* was slowing down.

Mrs. Rentley had said there were visitors coming aboard. This motor boat must be bringing them. Where had it come from? Was it from Las Palmas? It certainly must be from some place in the Canaries.

Whom could it be bringing? She stood close to the open porthole, listening, but in the confusion of sound could distinguish nothing to enlighten her.

From the safe gloom of the forecastle Grant Rushton also watched. Keeler had brought him certain information about what had transpired at the last meeting in the saloon, but that was little.

It was not until Rushton saw the Countess Saladier's head appear above the side and watched her spring lightly to the deck that he began to guess something of the truth.

But that guess didn't approach closely until, to his angry amazement, he saw the unconscious form of Sir Charles Gilson swung over the side and carried off.

Scarcely had he grasped this fact than he got a fresh jolt. It was the appearance of Frick as he clambered on to the deck and turned to wait for Count Saladier. Then came the two French gunmen whom Rushton had seen on board the *Corsair*.

Rushton drew back still farther into the darkness. It was obvious enough that Sir Charles had been brought along by force. But it was equally plain that Frick had come as an ally of the Saladiers.

All the doubt he had had of Frick rushed back upon him. It was obvious enough now how the Saladiers had become so well informed of the movements of Sir Charles and the plans.

It also looked as though, whatever differences had existed between the Rentley and the Saladier gangs on board the *Corsair*, they were on friendly enough terms now.

It wasn't difficult for Rushton to put two and two together and find the correct total. He could trace how it had all come about. The connecting link was the vital part of the plans that only Sir Charles could supply. His own position that had been strengthened by his statement that he could supply that vital part would have collapsed in any event. It was well for him that he had made his getaway when he did.

But now, instead of only Mrs. Rentley, Ricardo and the two van Korsens to deal with, he had the Saladiers and their two gunmen, as well as Frick. And Rushton was beginning to think that Frick was going to prove the toughest of the lot.

The whole gang vanished from the deck. Rushton was nursing his knees when Keeler appeared. The moment he loomed through the doorway, Rushton grabbed him.

"Did you see that?" he demanded in a low tone.

"Yes, I saw it, boss. That must be what they were talking about this morning. It isn't going to make matters any easier for you, is it?"

"Don't you worry, and don't you start getting ideas, Keeler. It might be unhealthy for someone. They're bound to have a palaver in the saloon now. I've got to hear what goes on. Get me some old clothes into which I can change—and some oily rags. I'll do the rest."

Suddenly he caught sight of a drunken fellow reeling across the deck. Over one eye he wore a black patch. Rushton caught Keeler's arm just as he was turning away.

"And bring me that black patch," he hissed.

Down in the saloon things were settling down into the palaver that Rushton had said would take place. There had been a certain amount of jockeying about at first, but the rival parties soon began coming to terms.

The two women might not feel much affection for each other, but they regarded each other with a certain respect. The countess was remembering what Mrs. Rentley had done singlehanded on board the *Corsair*. Mrs. Rentley was perfectly aware that the other woman was the brains of her gang.

Within a few minutes, Frick had assumed the chairmanship of the meeting. He sat at the end of the table in Muller's old seat. And it wasn't long before he knew the full story of how Muller had met his death. He smiled satirically at Mrs. Rentley.

"I'm afraid he spoofed you completely, my dear woman," he said. "And, knowing Grant Rushton, it is difficult for me to believe that he is dead."

"Then he's a mighty swimmer," she snapped. "And don't 'dear woman' me. I've run my end of things very well without any suggestions from you."

"Don't let us open things unpleasantly," put in the countess smoothly.

Frick was about to say something further when the door was flung open and three repellent figures lounged in. They were Keeler and Jonas, the nigger, who had been there on other occasions, and with them was another fellow, a murderous looking ruffian in dirty rags and with one evil eye glittering at the assembled party. The other eye was concealed by a black patch.

Frick and the Saladiers stared in astonishment at the sight. Frick half-rose as if to protest, but Ricardo touched his arm. He said something quickly in a low tone while Frick sank back, frowning and the three ruffians at the door grinned impudently.

Then Frick gave a grunt of disgust.

"Well, it isn't for me to criticise how you run your crowd, but I wouldn't have this sort of thing," he muttered.

"Wouldn't you, mister?" demanded Keeler. "You ain't getting any idea that this is your ship, are you? You can easily go back the way you came, you know."

Ricardo grinned at Keeler and kicked Frick under the table.

"All right, Keeler, all right," he said placatingly, our friend doesn't quite understand how things are. You can listen if you want to but I don't see what use it is."

"We'll listen all right, mister," returned Keeler ungraciously, and his two companions grinned widely.

Then the palaver went on, although it was plain enough that Frick and the Saladiers were cramped a bit by the presence of the three by the door.

It was soon equally plain that neither side was going to yield an inch. Ricardo, with a suavity that displayed more capability than one would have thought he possessed, politely but firmly made the case for the *Santa Cruz* gang.

"It must be acknowledged," he said, "that we have more to offer than you. We have the ship, fully equipped. We are in a position to act in full force if necessary." He made no mention of the fact that the main portion of the plans had vanished.

"Quite so, monsieur," rejoined the countess, "but it must be remembered that we hold the person of the one man who is vital to the completion of those plans."

"And he is on board this ship," came back Ricardo.

The countess smiled coldly.

"I hope that doesn't mean what it might imply, monsieur. You will understand that we weighed all the possibilities before we came. It is true that this ship is yours, but I would remind you that we, too, control a ship with a large number of men who are ready to act at a moment's notice. I speak of the former German cruiser that is already at the spot where the floating drome is being taken. And two of our men are on constant guard over the person you mention. They are, shall we say, excellent gunmen?"

"I don't think there need be any difference of opinion," put in Mrs. Rentley crisply. "I have a suggestion to make. Time is precious. If we are to bring matters to a successful finish we must act quickly. It is unlikely that the disappearance of Sir Charles Gilson will be accepted quietly. The Spanish authorities at Las Palmas will act. The British government will act. Every ship will be on the lookout. Then, too, we must not forget that his own ship, the *Corsair* is still in these waters. Therefore we must pull together. Do you not agree?"

A murmur of assent went round the table.

"I have a suggestion to make," she went on. "We have the man here on board. Let us make him an offer. If he listens to reason he shall be given his life. If he refuses our demands then we shall be compelled, for our own protection, to deal with him differently."

This, a concrete if daring suggestion, met with further approval and it was on this basis that the discussion went on. But, before it had gone very far there was an interruption. The door behind where Keeler and his two companions were standing was opened a few inches. Someone reached through and touched Keeler on the arm. Keeler slipped out and closed the door. But it opened a few moments later to re-admit him.

The talk at the table subsided. All eyes were turned towards the three ruffians. They saw Keeler mutter something to Jonas and the man with the patch over his eye. Then all three vanished through the door.

When they were gone Ricardo looked at the van Korsens and Mrs. Rentley.

"What's up?" he muttered. "I don't like the look of that."

"Probably the brutes are quarrelling again," Mrs. Rentley hazarded. And, certainly, it seemed as if she might be right, for now, from up above, came the sound of pistol shots.

CHAPTER XVI

THE leadership that Keeler had assumed among the six hundred criminals was, of itself, a flimsy thing.

He had organised a rough control which he ran somewhat after the fashion of a 'racket.'

His cunning brain, trained in all forms of trickery, had soon seen the possibilities of gaining power among the others through exercising a control of the food and drink supplies.

He had no trouble in gaining the adherence of half a dozen others, who, of course, would share in the plums that came the way of those who controlled things.

Nor were food and rum the only graft. The majority of those criminals had come aboard with varying sums of money—some, indeed, with considerable amounts.

It began to change hands rapidly, as is always the case among the type. With no dives and no women to spend it on they were forced to content themselves with drink and gambling.

Once they were away from Buenos Aires the South American authorities didn't care two straws what became of them. If they were refused a landing at European ports that would be just too bad. But one thing was certain, they would never be given permission to land again at any port in South America. If they gained secret admittance that was another matter.

It was a unique and daring experiment to deport hundreds of desperate criminals in such fashion. The ship had been equipped with stores and fuel for six months. At the end of that time the officers were at liberty to leave. It was hoped that the human cargo would have been scattered among various European ports. The hulk itself didn't matter. It was worth little having been refused insurance at Lloyd's except at prohibitive rates.

The whole thing had been a beautiful chance for the unscrupulous ring which Muller and Ricardo represented. In South America his principals had bought control of the *Santa Cruz* for the proverbial song. The officers had been only too pleased to relinquish their charge at Bordeaux with full pay, a substantial bonus and fares paid back to South America.

Here was a ship loaded with desperate ruffians who were ripe for anything. What Muller and Ricardo had to offer was not only excitement to break the enforced boredom under which they were chafing, but, better still, more money— with the chance of landing somewhere at last.

Hence they had been quite amenable at first. And, with the chance to purchase supplies of rum and cheap wine at Bordeaux, Keeler and his fellow grafters had established themselves in a position that promised well, becoming, at the same time, a sort of liaison party between their fellows and the after-guard.

Nevertheless, Keeler did not entirely control the racket without opposition. There were other brains as cunning as his and eyes as greedy.

Even before the coming of Muller and the Rentley gang, envious glances had been cast at Keeler's graft. The soil was ripe for mischief. It only needed the seed. And the seed was supplied with the launching of Keeler's campaign of whispering.

It was impossible to establish complete understanding without risk. Rushton had realised this when he first broached the matter to Keeler. But it was a risk that had to be taken.

The first sign that things were not running smoothly came that same afternoon when the three were in the saloon listening to the discussion there.

It was one of Keeler's men who had come down to warn him. On reaching the deck, it was plain enough to a man who had herded with that scum as Keeler had herded during the past months, that something was certainly wrong.

There were groups still gambling as usual, and the rum hogsheads were being patronised as freely as ever. But there was a subtle difference in the general disposal of the groups that Keeler spotted in a moment.

His cunning eye, trained to detect danger under such circumstances, lit on one group that was gathered for'ard. He made for it without the least hesitation. Rushton and Jonas, the nigger, kept close beside him. Rushton knew that the whole thing was likely to burst in a flash. He was not ready yet to have a showdown. He realised the peril of Sir Charles Gilson and Cara Hume if such a thing came now. The gangs would not hesitate to kill anyone to save their own skins. But he also realised that this was a thing Keeler must deal with. He must hide his own identity as long as possible.

And Keeler showed no hesitation in coming to the point. He kept on until he was close to the group, and the men now turned to watch him. Hands were hanging close to guns and knives. One big burly half-caste with vicious bloodshot eyes was obviously the leader. He was a fellow who had been at loggerheads with Keeler ever since the latter had neglected to make him a member of the inner circle of grafters.

Keeler stood and grinned at him. A sudden silence seemed to fall upon every group. The gamblers stopped play and watched. The men at the rum casks held their dippers and turned sly eyes upon the scene. Jonas, the nigger, was smiling broadly. He was a very dangerous man, was that nigger.

"What is this I hear?" asked Keeler softly. "Are you thinking of putting yourself up against me, Karbo?"

The half-caste hunched his shoulders forward.

"Who do you tink you are?" he demanded in high-pitched liquid tones that spoke of the negro blood in him. "Who dis feller, eh?" He indicated Rushton.

For answer, Keeler reeled off a string of blasphemous, scathing epithets that were scarcely above a whisper, and the names he called the half-caste made Karbo's piggy eyes contract with rage.

In a flash, Karbo's hand dropped to his gun and he drew with amazing speed. But Keeler was even quicker. The two guns crashed, seemingly, on the exact instant.

Rushton who had been standing with his arms hanging loosely against his hips, distinctly heard the thud of a bullet striking Keeler, but Karbo pitched forward on to his face, shooting again as he fell. The bullet struck the deck.

For a split second, Keeler stood swaying, then he lurched against Rushton. Two ruffians who had been beside Karbo were drawing their guns. Another fellow with a knife was leaping towards Rushton. Rushton held Keeler with one arm while he shot with the other.

Jonas, the nigger was still grinning broadly. And now, with a knife in one hand and a knuckleduster in the other, he broke out into a low chuckle that struck Rushton as a savage, sinister thing under such conditions.

Slash!

Swinging his great arm up in an arc, Jonas drove the knife-blade into the abdomen of the nearest gunman. Rushton felt suddenly sick at what followed.

Crack!

A ham-like hand that was gripping the knuckleduster crashed on to another attacker's skull, cracking it like an eggshell.

Jonas was laughing uproariously, his huge mouth showing white teeth and red gums.

"Dat's fo' Mandy," he sang, "and dat's for Jonas. Come on yo' white trash an' meet lil' Jonas friend."

Keeler had recovered. The bullet from Karbo's gun had ripped through his side. But he was able to shoot again, and, forming a grim contrast to Jonas, he went in with the gun blazing fast.

Those of the other gang who still stood on their feet broke and ran. Jonas followed them, laughing, but Keeler looked faint, and Rushton grabbed his arm.

"Come on, Keeler," he urged. "They're finished. What you need is a swig of rum."

Keeler yielded. Jonas came back and gave Rushton a hand. They got him along to one of the hogsheads and gave him a dipper of rum. Then they made their way into the fo'c'sle. But, just before they were hidden by its gloom, Rushton happened to turn and look back.

He saw Ricardo and Mrs. Rentley standing at the head of the main companion. Others were behind them. Then he caught sight of one of their late antagonists lurching towards them. He knew they were by no means finished with the outbreak that had been staged by Karbo. But Karbo would take no further part. Two of the convicts were already heaving his limp body over the side.

Keeler's wound was bleeding fast, but it was only a rip in the flesh. Jonas held the dipper of rum while Rushton sloshed the raw spirit into the open tissues. Then he found an old shirt and tore it into bandages.

While Rushton worked they talked in low tones.

"Someone will spill the stuff," he murmured. "Stand still, Keeler. And we've got a double mob to deal with now. How about it, Keeler? Are you going to stick?"

"I told you I'd come in, and I'll stay."

"How about Jonas?"

The negro's teeth showed white in the gloom. "Jonas stick all right, boss. You pay."

"I'll pay all right," Rushton assured him. "But I've got to change my plans. We've got to anticipate any move they might make. Go to the door, Jonas, and see what's happening."

The negro stood peering along the deck for some minutes. Then he returned, still grinning.

"Plenty happen, boss. Two of Karbo's gang just go down compan' with Ricardo."

"That means a split is certain. All right, we'll meet it. How soon can you tell me definitely, Keeler, the number we can depend on?"

"Jonas and I can move about now," responded Keeler with a wince of pain as Rushton hauled the bandage tight.

"All right. Get busy. Pin them down as soon as you can. You know what to offer. Double whatever the others have promised. It will be paid."

Keeler and Jonas moved off then, and Rushton sank back to think things out. He knew a crisis was at hand. The arrival of the Saladier gang was complication enough in itself, but bringing Sir Charles Gilson on board had made matters ever so much worse.

It would be difficult to choose between the two gangs. One was as ruthless as the other. Together they would be capable of any devilry, and, in the shuffle, it was quite on the cards that Sir Charles would be murdered out of hand.

Could he depend upon Keeler and Jonas? Would they be able to influence an appreciable number of the criminals? Only one thing would appeal to those ruffians—money. And there was only Keeler's word that Rushton would pay to convince them. Would they believe it?

It was a terrific gamble. He was throwing everything on to this one turn of the wheel. He made absolutely no count of himself. He had taken on the job, and he would stick. But Sir Charles—the girl, Cara Hume—the plans which were now stuffed under the bunk on which he sat—it was the very devil.

Yet, curiously enough, it wasn't from Ricardo, the van Korsens or the Count Saladier that he feared most. It was from the two women that he anticipated the most danger, and, of those two, he thought it likely that Mrs. Rentley was most to be watched.

The 'Orchid' might be classed as a rattle-snake. But Mrs. Rentley was as quick and deadly as a Russell's viper!

CHAPTER XVII

SIR CHARLES GILSON had not been as unconscious as he appeared when he was carried over the side of the *Santa Cruz*.

The doped pad which Frick had held over his mouth had done its work swiftly, but Sir Charles was a tough old war horse. Even though he had lost a good deal of blood from his head wound his iron constitution had battled amazingly well against the influence of the drug.

While still on board the motor boat the effects of the stuff had started to recede in waves that returned again and again to overwhelm his senses, but, each time, with lessening force.

His conscious knowledge of what was happening was still muddled. But somewhere within him there was a little tap-tap-tapping of caution that warned him to play possum until he was in a position to grapple with things.

Frick scrutinised him several times. Had he had the slightest suspicion that Sir Charles was not as completely 'out' as he seemed, he would have given him another dose of the stuff.

The victim didn't know just where he was being taken when he was hauled over the side of the *Santa Cruz*. He was only aware in a hazy way of his surroundings. But his brain was starting to function less intermittently, and when he was thrown on to a sofa in the music saloon he lay like one dead, trying to get some idea of what was happening.

It was thus that Cara Hume found him. She had been urged by Mrs. Rentley to take a little exercise in the corridor, and had reached the music saloon quite by chance.

She had never actually seen the shipping magnate on board the *Corsair*. But it did not need much deduction for her to guess his identity. She had overheard enough talk for that.

She crossed to him at once and knelt down, taking hold of his shoulders.

"Sir Charles, Sir Charles," she whispered.

Beneath lowered lids he had watched her cross the saloon. He couldn't quite fit her in with what he knew of either the Rentley or the Saladier gang. She didn't look that sort, and yet, he reflected, neither did Mrs. Rentley.

Her voice became urgent, and there was something in it that caused him to open one eye and regard her questioningly.

"You are Sir Charles Gilson?" she urged.

"I am. What do you want?"

"I am a friend—truly. I am being kept by force on board this dreadful ship."

"What ship is it?"

She told him in whispers. Both his eyes were open now and he was watching her intently. He knew all about the Ship of the Accursed that had been roaming the seas for months past.

"So this is where Rushton went with the woman," he muttered. Then he caught her arm. "What are you doing here? How did you get here?"

Again she explained.

"Where's Rushton then?" he asked her sharply.

"I don't know. Something happened. One of the gang was killed and the plans were taken. They say it was Mr. Rushton. They said, too, that he had dived over the side. But I have had a strange message. It was thrown in through the porthole of my cabin. It was signed with his initials. If it is genuine then he is still on board."

"So Rushton had to disclose his hand so soon," he muttered. "Have you heard what they want of me?"

"No. They are talking in the saloon now."

"That means the two gangs have joined forces. Well, I can guess what they want. And I can see now what Frick has been up to. You and I will have to work together, my dear. Do you know how you can get in touch with Rushton?"

"No. He just said he was still on board and that I was to be very careful, and to remain in my cabin as much as possible."

"Do you think it is true that he got hold of the plans?"

"Oh, yes, they were very upset. There was a lot of confusion and shooting, but he got away."

"You have told me something very important. They'll be after me soon. I'll know then what they are up to. You had better not take any risks, my dear. I'll try and keep in touch with you and we must make contact with Rushton if he is still on board. What was that?"

He had seen her head turn swiftly and her eyes grow wide with sudden fear as she stared towards the door. It had opened an inch or so, then it had closed gently. Someone had been spying and possibly listening, but who it was she could not tell.

She whispered her fear, and, rising, ran to the door. She threw it open and peered in both directions along the corridor. There was only one person visible some distance away. It was Mrs. Rentley coming towards her, smoking a cigarette and smiling oddly.

Something happened inside Cara Hume. Until this moment she had been, more or less, acquiescent to the force of circumstances. She had been so completely engaged with her own fears and terrors that she had possessed no confidence in her own puny powers to achieve anything against odds that seemed so overwhelming.

But now all fear for herself was submerged in a deep anger that had been born suddenly. It may have been inspired by the sight of a man of Sir Charles's age at the mercy of such brutal treatment. It may have been something less definite, a growing realisation within her that she too possessed powers of dissimulation.

Whatever it was she met Mrs. Rentley's stare indifferently.

"I have spoken to the man in there. Who is he?" she demanded.

"I think you know," drawled Mrs. Rentley.

"It is Sir Charles Gilson?"

"Of course. You found him conscious?"

"Not fully."

"And what, may I ask, did you say to him?"

"Nothing," lied Cara Hume glibly. "He is, I should say, just beginning to realise his surroundings."

At this moment the door of a cabin on her right opened and Ricardo appeared. He was smiling like one who is enjoying an inward joke. She guessed now that it had been he who had opened the saloon door and closed it again so gently.

He put his arm round her and drew her close. She conquered her violent distaste and desire to struggle. She even smiled a little as he looked down at her.

"Mustn't tell fibs, my dear," he said smoothly. "I think our friend is a little more conscious than that, no?"

"How can I tell?" she asked carelessly. "I tried to talk to him but he seemed dazed. See for yourself."

"We shall discuss this later, you and I," he promised her, still smiling.

Mrs. Rentley had been watching them closely.

"What does this mean?" she asked sharply.

"It means, dear lady, that we can now have a talk with our guest," he returned. "I suggest that this young woman should return to her cabin."

Cara Hume was only too glad to escape. But no sooner was she in her own cabin than she stood by the door listening. Presently she opened it a crack and peered along the corridor. She could see Ricardo supporting Sir Charles along towards the main saloon while Mrs. Rentley followed, a pistol in her hand.

She watched them until they disappeared into the saloon, then she withdrew into her cabin and locked the door. She knew she would never be permitted to go along and witness whatever devilry they were about to play upon their victim.

Nor was Grant Rushton present at that second gathering, which took place in the late afternoon. Since the trouble with Karbo he dared not expose himself too much to risk of scrutiny.

And neither Keeler nor Jonas could be there. He had sent them out to circulate again among the mob of criminals. He must discover without loss of time how far Karbo had got with his mischief.

So, in the gloom of the fo'c'sle, he tried to plan his next step. He was not regarding Mrs. Rentley or Ricardo now as his major problem. It was Frick with whom he must deal. Frick would never run the risk of allowing Sir Charles to go free now. Once he had come into the open he could never retreat. He would play his hand to the limit, and Rushton couldn't see a single hope for Sir Charles, whether he yielded to their demands or not.

He canvassed the possibility of reaching the wireless room and sending a general S.O.S. for assistance. But he realised that he would never be allowed to do so. He would be overpowered and killed out of hand before he could even get started.

Then there was the question of Sir Charles. How to get in touch with him? And the girl, Cara Hume? She was an additional worry. If he could use her somehow as a go-between he might manage something. But was she game? It might be worth trying. The gang might consider her of so little importance that she could become a point of contact.

He got out the bit of paper and pencil that Keeler had brought and wrote a cautious note. It was almost too dark to see by the time he had finished, and then Keeler and Jonas came in.

Down in the saloon, the gang that had gathered round the table were discovering that they had caught a tartar in Sir Charles. The moment he laid eyes on Frick he broke into a tirade of denunciation that would have blistered the deck of a windjammer.

But Frick only met it all with a smile. He held the whip hand just then, and knew it. And when Sir Charles paused, he stated his demands as coolly as if he were sitting in a London office and the thing was no more than an ordinary business deal.

"Of course you will refuse," he wound up curtly. "But you will change your mind. We have no time to waste. You will be given some hours to make your decision. If you still refuse— well, we shall know how to deal with you."

Sir Charles stared at him in glowering contempt and burst into a fresh tirade. But Frick only waved him away.

"You won't get anywhere with that sort of attitude, my dear sir," he told him. "You must realise that I am determined. I haven't taken this step without planning everything fully. You have until to-night to decide. That is all. Only let me warn you that unless you agree to our demands in full you will never leave this ship alive."

Sir Charles was dragged along to a cabin and locked in. It was almost directly across from Cara Hume's cabin. She watched anxiously and listened while the key was turned.

It was dark now. In her hand she held something that had been thrown in through her cabin porthole as before. But it was no more than a scribble addressed to her and it enclosed another note.

"Get this to Sir Charles if possible," was all it said.

And now she asked herself how she was going to manage to do so. She could hear a sound as of a key being withdrawn from a lock, then footsteps disappeared along the passage.

She opened her door and peered out cautiously. The corridor seemed to be empty. She knew, however, that someone might appear at any moment. Her heart was racing painfully as she slipped outside across to the other door. She was not certain that Sir Charles was there but it was her only chance. Bending down, she pushed the bit of paper under the door as far as possible. As she rose she rapped her knuckles hurriedly on the panel, then she sped back to her own cabin.

Peering over her shoulder she had just time to distinguish a figure in the distance before she softly closed her own door. She could not tell whether she had been seen or not.

She could not tell whom it could be. It had not seemed bulky enough for Ricardo. She had never seen Frick. But she had, of course, caught glimpses of the Saladiers on board the *Corsair*. It wasn't a woman and it was too tall for the podgy count. It might be one of the van Korsens or someone else who had come aboard that day with the Saladiers.

She listened close to her door. The footsteps seemed to pause outside, then, suddenly, the handle of her door was turned and the door flung open with such force that it sent her reeling backwards.

She recovered and stood swaying. The intruder switched on the light and she saw one who was a stranger to her. But there was that in his face and bearing that told her it was someone of consequence in the gang. It was Frick.

He closed the door and smiled coldly.

"I've heard about you, young woman, and I think it is time we got acquainted. I was sure you were listening at your door. What did you expect to discover?"

She eyed him coolly enough.

"Is there any reason why I should answer your questions?" she countered curtly.

"You will find there is every reason," he snapped. "You were watching the corridor. What was the interest? Was it Sir Charles Gilson? I'm not quite satisfied about things on board this ship. So, unless you wish to be kept locked in your cabin, you had better be frank with me."

"Who are you? By what right do you adopt this tone to me? If you wish to know anything about me, ask Mrs. Rentley or Senor Ricardo."

"What is the trouble?"

Ricardo had suddenly appeared in the passage from the saloon, making no noise on rubber-soled shoes. Cara Hume seized her chance. If she could create a difference, even a mild one, between any of the members of the gang, it might help.

She smiled at Ricardo as never before. She appealed to him as if she regarded him as her guardian.

"Have you given this man permission to force his way into my cabin and ask me questions?" she demanded of Ricardo.

Ricardo frowned. He was not anxious to quarrel with Frick or any others of the Saladier gang, but he didn't intend to have anyone poaching on his preserves. He considered that he had shown great restraint in postponing his lovemaking until a more favourable time.

"What's the idea, Frick?" he asked quickly. "Miss Hume is in my care. What is the reason of this?"

Frick smiled coldly.

"There are too many women in this thing," he returned curtly. "I'm not satisfied that this young miss is as harmless as she seems. She was spying in the corridor when I came along. I was questioning her."

"Well, I'll do any questioning of her that there is to do," growled Ricardo. "You can leave her alone. She has no part in the other matter."

Frick uttered a sound that was like the sharp hissing of a snake as he jerked his head towards Ricardo.

"Listen," he said in a voice scarcely above a whisper, "I am not in this thing for fun. You had better understand that. I'm not satisfied about Rushton, and I'm not satisfied about this girl. I'm going to test every string to-night and then I'm going to do some pulling. You'd better not interfere."

"Are you threatening me?" roared Ricardo. "You'd better remember who runs this show. I do. I control the money and I give the orders. And don't forget I control the ship, too."

"For the moment you may. But we needn't quarrel over the matter. I want to see you and Mrs. Rentley alone. We've got to settle what is to be done. And I'll see that that old fool Gilson gives us the key plan we need. Come with me."

Together they left the cabin. Cara waited until they were in the passage, then closed the door and again stood against it. She listened until she thought they must have reached the saloon. She peered out but could see no one.

Across the passage a line of light showed under the door of the cabin into which Sir Charles had been thrust. She slipped out and stole across to it.

As she expected, the door was locked. She tapped lightly, then, bending down, she pushed the note under as far as possible.

She had just straightened up when a door opened and light shone along the passage. She fled back to her own cabin and closed the door, locking it.

Again she stood listening. She thought she could hear voices in the distance. The door of the saloon must be open. Had anyone seen her?

She started nervously as, without warning, there came a sharp tapping at her door. She voiced a whisper.

"Who is it?"

"I—Ricardo. Open, I want to speak to you."

She turned the key. She knew it would be useless to refuse. It would take very little time to smash in the door.

He pushed in and caught her by the shoulder.

"Now then, what is the truth of this?" he demanded. "I want it all. I've been too easy with you. What tricks are you up to?"

She deliberately made her voice stupid and sullen.

"I don't know what you are talking about."

"Oh, yes you do. Frick is right. I've stood enough from him and I saw you myself at that other door. What were you doing there? Come on, out with it."

"You're hurting me."

He bent his head until his face was close to hers, then he swore softly.

"I've made a mistake. But it isn't too late to rectify it. I'll take care you don't get a chance to fool me again. You've fooled us all making us think you were such a simple miss."

His breath was on her cheek, his eyes were suddenly hot and purposeful. She shrank back, trying to push him away from her. He only laughed, so futile were her efforts. Then the laugh vanished and something came into his eyes that filled her with a real terror. She struggled with all her strength while he held her and forced her back towards the bunk. She tried to scream, but he put a big, soft hand over her mouth.

Then she saw something that closed her throat more effectually than that hand.

From round the frame of the open doorway, came another hand that gripped a knife. Part of an arm came into view. Then she saw the hand go up, come down, then go up again and vanish as swiftly as it had come. Ricardo gave a grunt that rose to a curious treble whistle. Then he slid to the floor and lay flat on his face.

She was still standing in frozen horror, gripping the edge of the bunk to support her trembling limbs, when Mrs. Rentley appeared in the doorway. Then she collapsed in a dead faint.

CHAPTER XVIII

WHEN Cara Hume recovered she was lying on her bunk. Mrs. Rentley was sitting beside her. Ricardo's body had disappeared. Mrs. Rentley was holding a bottle of smelling salts under her nostrils. She did not notice at first that Mrs. Rentley was sitting so that she partly faced the door, and that a pistol was lying in her lap.

"So you've come round, have you?" she heard the other saying. "Now you and I are going to have a little talk. Don't shudder. There isn't time for that sort of thing and it is a little too much from one as deep as you are. Now then, come across, you little devil. Who killed Ricardo?"

"I don't know."

Cara Hume hardly knew her own voice, but, even though her wits were still muzzy, she was telling herself that she must be careful.

"Don't lie to me. I saw enough to know differently. You held Ricardo while your accomplice stabbed him in the back. It wasn't the old fool. I know he was in his cabin. Was it Rushton?"

"I tell you I don't know. I didn't see."

Mrs. Rentley lit a cigarette and puffed rapidly for a few moments. Then, swiftly, viciously, she jammed the burning end of the tube into Cara Hume's throat. The girl shrank away with a cry as the fire bit into the flesh, but the other struck her hard across the face.

"That's just a warning," she said pleasantly as she withdrew the crushed cigarette and went on puffing at it. "Now then, who was it?"

"I tell you I don't know. I didn't see. I only saw a hand and an arm."

"Well, did you recognise that? It would be the right hand, I suppose. What sort of a hand was it, white or black?"

"White, I think. I only caught a glimpse of it. It was very dirty."

"You know, my dear, you'd better be frank with me. I've been suspecting for some time that our slippery friend Rushton never went over the side at all. I believe he is still on board, and I'm going to learn the truth."

"How should I know?"

"I'll tell you. I was on deck when I saw that ruffian, Keeler, go over the side just above your cabin. He had a scraper in his hand as if he were going to do some small job. I didn't think much of it at the time, but I've been putting two and two together since then. Unless you come across with the truth I'm going to strip you and search you from head to foot. I won't have to call for help unless you force me to do so. Which is it?" Cara remembered the two notes from Rushton that were still inside her dress. They seemed proof—she must believe that he was still on board —in hiding and yet active. She could only hope fervently that Sir Charles had received the other note.

But Mrs. Rentley wasn't as sure as she pretended. She had probably got wind of something suspicious on deck. She was a very shrewd and clever woman. And very desperate just now. But she didn't *know* anything definite about Rushton. She was only pumping and trying to make her (Cara) betray herself. Well, two could play at that game.

"You can do that, of course," Cara said at last, wearily. "I am quite at your mercy. That is what Ricardo thought. But I tell you I do not know who attacked him. I did not see. But you should know from one thing that it wasn't Grant Rushton."

The other woman's eyes flashed with sheer jealousy as she heard the girl use his full name.

"Well," she said dangerously, "why wasn't it?"

"You know he would never stab a man in the back like that."

"I believe you have more sense than I gave you credit for. Look here, I'm going to tell you something. If I hadn't seen Frick and the others in the saloon I'd have thought Frick did it. I know that he and Ricardo had a difference. It was over you, wasn't it?"

"Not over me. It took place here. That strange man, Frick you call him, was bullying me. Ricardo took exception to it. That is all."

"And then minutes later Ricardo is killed. Now listen. I believe Grant Rushton is on board, and I believe you are in touch with him. I don't trust that fellow Keeler. Then there was some trouble this afternoon on deck. There was a killing. I believe Rushton is working among the crew. Frick and the Saladiers don't know that yet. But—" and here she leant forward, speaking in a lower tone—"I don't trust that crowd. I believe Frick is trying to double-cross us. I'm going to give you a message to get through to Rushton for me. Tell him that I am still ready to talk business with him, that I don't hold anything against him, and that if he will make a deal with me I'll play square."

Cara Hume realised suddenly that circumstance had thrown her into a stronger position than she could have hoped to achieve through her own efforts. She saw that she held an advantage here that she might turn to the profit of Rushton and Sir Charles if she played her cards properly. But could she do so against such a finished player as Mrs. Rentley.

"Do you think he would believe that—I mean if all you say about him being still on board is true?"

Mrs. Rentley eyed her savagely.

"I don't know just what I'd better do about you," she said at last. "I'm making a fair offer to Rushton. If he comes in I'm willing to spring a trap on the Saladiers. I can't pull together with this man Frick. Maybe you didn't have anything to do with the murder of Ricardo. I don't believe you've got the spirit. Maybe Frick fixed it some way. At any rate, Muller is gone, and now Ricardo. That leaves only me and the van Korsens, and they're not much good. Besides, Ricardo had the money. If Rushton will rejoin me I'll see that Sir Charles is all right. I want my share, that's all. Think that over and let him know. I've got to go now. Don't you spill anything to Frick and the Saladiers or I'll slit your throat."

And Cara Hume knew that, though the tone was quiet, the threat was real enough.

She left the cabin abruptly. The moment she was gone, Cara Hume rolled off the bunk. Then she fumbled inside her dress until she found the two screwed-up bits of paper that were Rushton's notes. She tore them quickly into bits and thrust them out of the porthole into the sea.

She stood thinking hard. She believed that Mrs. Rentley was sincere enough in some of what she had said.

So it was the Saladiers who had come aboard and brought Sir Charles. Already, it seemed, things were not working smoothly. She didn't know who Frick was. She had not heard his name before. But she could believe that he and Mrs. Rentley would soon clash.

She could see, too, how Mrs. Rentley's position had been further weakened by the murder of Ricardo. She shuddered afresh. It seemed impossible to believe that big, gross, oily Ricardo who had been able to terrify her so short a time before was actually dead. It didn't seem possible that a single knife-thrust could reach between those thickly-fleshed shoulder-blades to the heart. But then she remembered how he had slumped to the floor.

But who had killed him? Not until Mrs. Rentley had questioned her had she had a chance to think about the hand that had held the knife.

112

Could it have been Rushton's? It was a big hand, a firm hand, and it had been covered with dirt. But would Rushton use a knife to kill? It seemed alien to the nature of such a man that he would give a knife-thrust in the back. It would have been more like him to slam Ricardo on the head with a gun.

Then she recalled that, in the brief moment during which the hand had been poised above Ricardo's back, she had seen a ring shining against the tightly drawn skin. She thought it was a silver ring, a large, thick ring with some kind of a head fashioned in it.

Yes, she was more and more sure. Well, that was a clue. The person who had killed Ricardo had worn such a ring. She would know if she saw it again.

But why had he done the deed? Was it to protect her? Cara Hume did not think there was anyone on board who would go to such extremes to protect her unless it was Rushton (she was thinking of Rushton very differently now) and she had already told herself that he would not have struck in that fashion.

Then who? And for what purpose? Was it, as Mrs. Rentley seemed to half suspect, that Frick had arranged it? Was he already cutting off his allies one by one so that he could take their share of the profits?

If so, might it not be a good thing if Grant Rushton knew this as soon as possible? She did not know what Mrs. Rentley had meant by saying that there was trouble among the criminals. She had hinted that Rushton had been at work among them. She must be strongly suspicious to be so definite.

And Sir Charles, where would he come out of all this intrigue and counter-intrigue?

It was amazing what a change had come over Cara Hume in the last hour or two. In fact, ever since receiving Rushton's first note, the change had begun. She was not thinking of herself or her own peril now. She was thinking of Grant Rushton and, of course, Sir Charles.

She was still trying to decide what to do when she saw the door begin to open. She started to rush towards it, but she was too late to prevent entry.

Then her eyes widened as a hand appeared, a hand that was begrimed with dirt and on one finger of which was a thick silver ring with the shanks twisted up into a head of some sort. It was the hand that had sent Ricardo to his death.

No face appeared. The hand turned upwards and beckoned. Despite herself she moved forward in obedience. Then, quickly, the fingers caught the switch and turned out the light. She felt a touch on her arm. She was grasped and drawn into the corridor. Then something was thrown about her and she could make little resistance against the strength that propelled her towards the 'midships companion.

In the saloon, the crooks were again gathered about the table. But the balance of strength had altered materially.

A few hours before, the Saladier gang had been in the position of suitors willing to offer any terms in order to gain a foothold in the *Santa Cruz*. Their most valuable contribution had been the person of Sir Charles Gilson.

But now Frick wore the manner of a dictator, with the 'Orchid' hanging on his every word and backing him up. The count echoed her. Frick was of far more value to the Saladiers than the Brown Priest had ever been.

Mrs. Rentley was playing almost a singlehanded game. The van Korsens had become almost nonentities since Muller's death. They might or might not be on her side in a violent showdown.

But she knew that, if she were to regain control of her former position she would need all her wits about her. She was perfectly confident now that Frick and the Saladiers were out to double-cross her. She could see the whole thing slipping away from her—all she had fought for and all she had killed men for.

She was more and more convinced that Rushton was still on board. She did not know the strength of his position, but she had a healthy respect for his nerve and brains. He had struck hard and sure while in the complete power of his enemies, and he had won a temporary victory.

How to retrieve her position? It was useless to try and use her feminine wiles upon Frick. If he had any weakness that way it was inclined towards the 'Orchid.'

What would be her position if they did succeed in forcing her out entirely? It would be unenviable, to say the least.

She weighed the chances of making a ruthless attack with her gun. The odds against her were too heavy. If she could make contact with Rushton would he listen to her? Or could she get control of Sir Charles and play him off as a strong card?

She had tested Cara Hume. The girl was more of a factor than she had dreamed. There was something queer there, but she couldn't quite put her finger on it. She would follow that up later in the evening. But now she must give her keen attention to what Frick was saying.

"I've got the strength of this mob on board," he was telling them. "They need control and I'm going to give it to them. We are past Teneriffe now. In three days we should overtake the floating drome at its anchorage. And our own crowd is already there waiting."

Mrs. Rentley knew he was referring to the former German cruiser that had been used by the financial crowd for whom the Saladiers had been working in an effort to establish a temporary ocean station. She had forgotten that for the moment. Now she realised that she would be completely defeated if Frick could swing both crowds together.

"Someone has been at work here," he went on. "Those fellows want action. They've had nothing but promises. I'm going to give them what they want. And I'm going to do something else. I'm going to have Sir Charles Gilson in here now and set him to work. There is going to be no more hedging. He can take his choice. If he doesn't set to work at once and turn out what we need then he's going over the side and we'll manage without him. Is that agreed?"

There was a murmur of assent. Mrs. Rentley said nothing. She was thinking faster than ever.

Frick rose.

"Come on then," he said curtly. "Let's get him."

The 'Orchid' and the count rose with him. The two van Korsens, after a glance at Mrs. Rentley, followed suit. Mrs. Rentley saw the two apache gunmen standing by the door. Keeler and Jonas were not there. It seemed ominous that they were absent. She realised that she was already alone. Frick was looking at her coldly. She smiled easily and got to her feet.

"A very good suggestion," she drawled. "Let us follow it."

But she knew, even as she uttered the words, that she had already been isolated.

Frick led the way along the passage to the cabin into which Sir Charles had been thrust. He rapped on the door and called. There was a light inside under the door, but no answer came.

Frick did not knock a second time. He caught the handle and gave it a twist as if he expected the door to be locked. But it wasn't. It opened easily and Frick started to enter. But he drew up quickly with an oath.

The cabin was empty.

CHAPTER XIX

RICARDO'S attack upon Cara Hume had complicated Rushton's plans.

Had he known where Sir Charles was confined he would never have sent the note through her. But not even Keeler had been able to ascertain where Sir Charles was imprisoned.

The note to Sir Charles was but a preliminary warning for him to be ready. Rushton had determined to hazard everything on quick action.

When Keeler returned to report that he had safely delivered the note to the girl, Rushton waited until full dusk. Then he, Keeler and Jonas made their way among the groups of criminals towards the 'midships companion.

Rushton's watchful eyes noted the change in the atmosphere. There was less gambling, more drinking and a good deal more talking among the criminals. It wasn't difficult to guess that some insidious force was at work, and it was equally easy to identify it with Frick and the Saladiers.

But no one attempted to obstruct them. The recollection of what had happened to Karbo was too vivid. Moreover, Keeler still controlled a large number of the toughest characters, and these were scattered at strategic points among the others.

The whole atmosphere was electric, however. A storm was brewing, and would break before long, though Rushton didn't know yet about the growing differences among the two gangs of crooks.

His immediate objective was to get hold of Sir Charles and Cara Hume and bring them along to the retreat he still controlled—the fo'c'sle. Then he intended to put the thing to a test. He knew that once the lid did blow off, Sir Charles and the girl would be in deadly peril from more directions than one.

They reached the corridor of the main deck without meeting a soul. It was, however, just as Ricardo made his fatal visit to Cara Hume, and immediately after she had been threatened by Frick. Had Rushton seen Frick then, the whole thing would have ended swiftly.

The three were standing in the gloom at the end of the passage when they saw Ricardo approach the girl's cabin. Rushton touched Keeler on the arm.

"Get him," he whispered.

He had not intended that order to mean what followed. Ricardo as a live hostage was worth more than a dead load.

But Keeler waited for no more. He reached the door of the cabin just as Ricardo was forcing the girl back on to her bunk. He struck swiftly. Then the opening of the saloon door caused him to draw back and retreat.

It was Mrs. Rentley, and Rushton realised that an uproar now might precipitate matters too soon, so he kept back.

But the moment Mrs. Rentley returned to the saloon, he and his two companions moved forward. Keeler opened the door of the girl's cabin, and it is known how he drew her out.

Rushton had his lips close to her ear while Keeler was throwing a voluminous oilskin about her.

"Be quiet," he warned her. "It's Rushton. Where is Sir Charles?"

She indicated the cabin where Sir Charles had been thrust. Keeler passed her along to Jonas. He then followed Rushton to the door of the other cabin.

It was locked. Rushton spoke in a low tone to Sir Charles. It was impossible to open the door from the inside. Rushton posted Keeler to meet any discovery from the saloon and searched for a key. He took the one from the door of Cara Hume's cabin and tried it in the other lock. It turned easily. One key would fit any of those doors.

In a moment he had the door open. Sir Charles stood staring until he recognised Rushton. Then he muttered two words.

"Good fellow."

"Come on, sir."

"Anything you say, Rushton. I'm ready."

Rushton drew him out into the corridor and closed the door. He put another oilskin about his shoulders and hurried him along the passage. They reached the deck. A thin fog coming in from the south of Teneriffe made things easier. They slipped along close to the side and among piles of litter until they were forward of the bridge. Then they dived into the fo'c'sle.

There were a good dozen of Keeler's men in the place now. He had been gradually drawing them together as a nucleus. Jonas the nigger was out on the deck somewhere circulating among the others.

Rushton had fixed up the narrow end of the fo'c'sle as well as possible for Sir Charles and the girl. There was a bulkhead here close to the stem which could be made into a sort of separate compartment.

A hurricane lantern hung from a nail, and by the poor light of this they were busy getting things straightened out when Jonas came in. He was grinning widely as usual. Both hands were full of guns he had collected somewhere.

Behind him came another figure that moved so shadowlike that no one noticed it. All eyes were on Jonas, who was joking while he tumbled the guns into an empty bunk.

The smaller figure slipped along in the shadow towards the bulkhead behind which Rushton was engaged with Sir Charles. It showed for a moment under the light of the lantern, a dark, indistinct blur. Then it vanished from view.

Rushton paused in what he was saying and turned his head. He thought someone was behind him. He could see nothing but his own bunk just round the curve of the stem. He peered round. All he saw was the crowd at the other end of the fo'c'sle gathered round Jonas.

He turned back. Had he been a little slower to do so he would have seen a thin shadow detach itself from the black in the space between his bunk and the one above. And then he would have lost it as it slid along the more dimly lit part of the fo'c'sle.

But some warning kept nagging at him. He got up and went to his bunk. Quickly he thrust a hand into the place where he had thrust the plans. They were gone.

He twisted and looked suspiciously at the gang by the door. He saw something small glide along the wall and go through the door quickly. He sprang to his feet and raced after it.

Keeler gave a shout. Rushton pulled up for a moment.

"Come here, quick, Keeler."

When the other reached him he grabbed his arm.

"Listen, I've got to go out. You're in charge. If anything happens before I get back, hold this place at all costs. I depend on you. I don't expect to be more than a few moments. Keep Jonas and the others with you."

Before Keeler could question him he was gone.

He burst out of the fo'c'sle to find that the fog had thickened. The flares along the deck were only indistinct blurs. He could see nothing of the person who had got away with the plans.

He stumbled over a coil of rope and reached the side. Then he stood listening as there came the sound of a shot, muffled in the fog.

Rushton knew that, before the mob of criminals had been shipped from South America, both the forward and the after holds had been roughly fitted up for their reception. Several hundreds of rough cubicles had been knocked up, and the majority of the criminals used these when they took the trouble to go below at all.

He had noticed that the hatches were always off, but, then, the weather had been consistently fine. In heavy weather the hatches would, of course, have to be closed, but whether the criminals would consent to be battened down below was another matter.

He had taken this condition into account when he was forming his plans. It had been part of his scheme to batten down the hatchways on those of the criminals he could not count upon. It would then be a simple matter to keep them under control.

But he was to find that someone else had had the same inspiration and that the initiative was out of his hands. That shot was the signal for an outbreak that began aft and spread like magic throughout the ship.

While Rushton grasped the side, startled by the suddenness of it all, a hurricane of shots, yells screams and curses broke upon him.

He turned and tried to reach the fo'c'sle. Through the fog a wedge of men rushed, carrying him back against the side with terrific violence.

It was impossible to tell friend from foe. He dared not reveal his own identity at that moment. He could only trust to Keeler to defend the fo'c'sle.

He dragged out his gun and made another effort to reach his objective. Someone cannoned into him. He felt a hand grasp his arm. He turned to strike, and then, as he was grasped again, he knew the other was a woman.

He caught hold of her, thinking at first that Cara Hume had followed him. A break in the swirling fog enabled him to get a brief glimpse of her features. It was Mrs. Rentley, and now, suddenly, he knew who had taken the plans.

But if he recognised the woman so did she know him despite the disguise he still wore. She had seen him clearly enough in the fo'c'sle and had heard him speak.

Her cloak came away in the struggle. Rushton felt his hands catching at stockinette that clung like a skin to her body. She was wearing nothing but the acrobatic suit that she had worn on board the *Corsair*.

She fought savagely to get one hand free. Rushton felt the hard

120

metal of a gun against his ribs. He struck her arm aside with a force that made her give a smothered cry of pain. Then he got a hold on her wrist, twisted her arm and caught hold of the gun.

He wrenched it from her grasp and held her so that she could not struggle.

"Don't be a fool," he warned her, "this deck will be a shambles soon. Here, up with you."

There was a boat hanging on davits close to where they stood. Rushton found the canvas cover loose enough to force aside. He tumbled the woman in and scrambled over beside her. He was still clutching her cloak and, as he felt something lumpy against his hand, he dug inside it. A low chuckle broke from him as his fingers grasped a packet of papers that he knew must be the plans.

He was surprised that she did not struggle but, surprisingly, she caught his head and drew it down.

"What is happening?" he heard her ask.

"Listen! There's the devil to pay aft. They'll be through here in force soon."

There wasn't much shooting now. The fog was too thick. But the cursing and scuffling was sinister proof that a desperate fight was in progress.

There came a high-pitched cry that died away slowly. It had burst very close to them. Rushton knew that someone had pitched down the open hatch.

It would have been sheer foolish heroics to plunge into that confusion, and Rushton knew it. His chief desire was to get back to the fo'c'sle and take control there. But he could not understand why an outbreak had come so soon unless Mrs. Rentley had inspired it. He knew that Keeler wasn't responsible, though now that the lid had blown off he thought it might be as well to let things run to a finish. But he had no intention that the woman now in his power—the 'tiger-woman' he had dubbed her privily—should get back to her base. Yet he was puzzled at her presence here at such a time, that she should have chosen such a moment to make her daring raid on the fo'c'sle.

"We can't stay here," he heard her protesting as she squirmed beside him.

"Why not?" he demanded. "This is as good a place as any, and I can make sure that you are up to none of your tricks. Presently I'm going to lug you along to the calaboose."

"Listen, you're being a fool," she panted, struggling harder than ever. "If we stay here we'll be caught like rats in a trap. Let's get back to the fo'c'sle if you want to. I didn't start this, I tell you. It must have been Frick."

"It's all the same thing," he growled as he forced her down again. "You or Frick or the Saladiers are all one."

"We are not. Frick and I have split. If you've spoken to the Hume girl you must know."

"That horse won't run here, my friend."

She gave up struggling.

"All right, have it your own way," she said more quietly. "But you will find your mistake. I've told you the truth. It was a mistake on our part to make a deal with Frick. If you hadn't killed Muller it would have been different. And then Ricardo. I can't even depend on the van Korsens. I tell you Frick and the Saladiers have double-crossed me. I told the Hume girl to tell you I'd work with you if you would make a deal. And I meant it. You fooled me all right, and you've got strong cards yet. But Frick is dangerous. It hasn't taken him long to start things among the mob. But I've got something yet to offer."

The sounds of the melee had died away somewhat. The fighting seemed to have become concentrated in the after-part of the ship, and, while listening to the woman with one part of his mind, Rushton had been debating the chances of getting Keeler and making a rush from the fo'c'sle. But her last words caught his full attention.

"What can you offer, conceding, for the sake of argument, that you are telling the truth?"

"Frick doesn't control the navigating crew on the bridge. They are still my men. They will do what I say. If you make a deal with me I'll swing them and we'll settle Frick. Then we can come to terms and I'll pull out."

Despite the critical position Rushton had to laugh.

"You've certainly got one priceless nerve. You remind me of a man going to the gallows telling the hangman he'll make him a present of the rope if he lets him off."

"Jeer if you wish. Time is short. I'll settle with you some other time for the way you fooled me. But just now I'm willing to postpone that in order to get Frick. There isn't another man to whom I'd make that offer. I could have killed you in the fo'c'sle if I had wished. But I didn't. Make this deal with me and you won't regret it. If you don't, Frick will get you and Sir Charles. He daren't let either of you escape now and you know it."

What she said was true enough. Now that Frick had come out into the open it would never do for him to let Sir Charles or Rushton get away with that knowledge. It was either he or they.

But was she bluffing? Was this all just to get away? Or was it true that she and Frick had split?

There was strength in what she said about the navigating crew on the bridge. They would be of importance to whoever controlled the ship. But, remembering what had happened on board the *Corsair*, and what she must be feeling towards him for the way in which he had fooled her, Rushton was wise to be cautious. It was an indication of how he regarded her that he considered her more dangerous than all the others put together.

Rushton was not left to make the final decision. There came a lull in the fighting forward and, in its freakish way, the fog cleared suddenly.

Then through the gangways beneath the bridge came a rush of men, shouting, cursing, filling the air with appalling oaths that were not drowned by the sharp clatter of pistols.

Rushton saw Keeler at the entrance to the fo'c'sle. He had a gun in his hand and was peering about. The light of the nearest flare lit up his evil countenance clearly. Then the black face of Jonas appeared over his shoulder. He was still grinning.

Rushton heaved himself up.

"Listen," he said curtly, "you're probably lying like sin, but I'm going to take a chance. Play in with me and you won't regret it. I tell you Frick can't win now anyway. He's got to go under if it takes everything we've got. If you stick with him it won't make any difference in the end. That's all."

"Wait."

She grasped him by the arm so hard that her nails dug into the flesh.

"What is it?" He was impatient to be gone for the fight was coming closer every moment.

"Are you in love with that chit of a girl?"

He cursed softly.

"What a place to ask a question like that. You must be crazy."

She let go and thrust him to the edge of the boat.

"Go on," she said curtly. "I've always fought alone. I can do so now."

He waited no longer. Sliding over the side of the boat he gave the canvas tarpaulin a jerk to pull it to the edge. Then he dropped to the deck and raced for the fo'c'sle just as the fighting mass of men gave before a violent rush which Rushton could not see.

He gave one look back at the boat just as he reached the entrance and Keeler hauled him inside, but he saw nothing of Mrs. Rentley. The cover lay just as he had left it.

CHAPTER XX

VESTA RENTLEY remained hidden in the boat.

She had played her last and best card with Rushton and thought she had lost.

All about her the fight was surging and, more than once, a bullet came crashing through the side of the boat. But the woman lay curled up in the bottom, careless, it would seem, of being hit.

It wasn't the first time she had been in a desperate position. She had always lived dangerously, with usually a profit substantial enough to repay her for the risks she took.

She knew her power over men and had always used it to the limit. Her experience had caused her to hold them in contempt—most of them. That did not apply to the defunct Muller or Grant Rushton.

She did not try to tell herself that she had conceived a *grande passion* for Rushton. She was too logical and direct for that sort of weakness. But there is no doubt that she felt for Rushton something she had never quite experienced before and, what made her angry with herself, still felt it despite his treatment of her. Every woman will always fall for some one man if she meets him. She had met Rushton.

She realised now, however, that she could not get Rushton to pull her chestnuts out of the fire for her. Of course, the offer to play in with him had been genuine only up to a point. She would have formed a liaison with the devil just then if it had meant dislodging Frick from the position he had so coolly appropriated.

With the death of Muller and the more recent killing of Ricardo everything had slipped away from her. She could not depend upon the van Korsens. They would follow the money.

Lone-handed she must try and wriggle through the complications and, whatever was done, must now be attempted on board this ship. All the ingredients were here—Sir Charles, the plans, Rushton, Frick and the Saladiers, not to mention the mob of criminals who were quite undependable.

Her final judgment was that Rushton was still her best bet. If she could reach and hold a position where she really possessed something worth while to offer she might make terms with him and Sir Charles, terms that might be far less attractive than what she had hoped to achieve, but, nevertheless, better than nothing at all.

Thus this woman without a nerve in her makeup figured her course while the fighting raged about her. She was not bothered in the least by any question of right or wrong. The word immoral could not have been applied to Vesta Rentley. She was simply amoral. And it would have been difficult to believe that she had a small daughter at a convent school in Belgium who adored the mother she thought was a teacher of physical culture in Paris.

She lifted the edge of the tarpaulin and peered out. The fog was coming down again, but she could still see by the light of the flares. It was difficult to understand how one faction could distinguish another, considering that they were all birds of a feather.

She knew that Frick had been busy that afternoon. She knew too that the two apache gunmen had been circulating among the criminals. It looked as though Frick had started a rush with those he knew he could depend upon and was counting on either beating the opposition into line or winning them over by persuasion. Once he was in complete control of the ship it would write finis to Rushton as well as to her schemes. But Frick didn't know for sure yet that she was going to pit her wits against his. He might mistrust her, but he probably thought she would be easy enough to deal with when the moment came.

The mass of the fighting had surged back towards the bridge, but now it reeled again towards her, and, at this same moment, she saw the man with the black eye patch, whom she knew to be Rushton, leap from the fo'c'sle a gun in each hand. Close behind him came Keeler and Jonas and then a pack of a dozen or so.

She watched to learn the effect of the rush. She expected to see them attack the rear of the men nearest but, instead of that, they pushed in among them and joined in repulsing the mob that was crowding through from the after-part of the ship.

No one had an eye for the boat in which she lay concealed. She slid over the edge and pulled her cloak about her. The fog was even more useful than the cloak. In a few minutes, if it continued to thicken, it would make it impossible for the two factions to tell which was which.

She kept close to the side and crept along until she was close to one flank of the melee. She had lost sight of Rushton since he had gone plunging into the thick of it. It occurred to her that now was the time to make for the fo'c'sle and force Sir Charles and the Hume girl back to their former cabins at the point of the gun. But with the new plan that was making in her mind she was as ready to have them in the fo'c'sle for the time being as directly under Frick's eye.

She reached the shadow of the bridge and caught hold of the uprights of an iron ladder. She went up this swiftly, her gun ready. Someone leapt after her and tried to drag her back. She swung her hand downwards and fired. The fellow dropped away.

She climbed higher and then found her way blocked by one of the navigating crowd who was standing grimly on bridge guard with a gun ready to blow the head off the first one that attempted to rush him. It was only Mrs. Rentley's quick voice that saved her.

Foord was the senior of the three navigating staff engaged by Muller for the job. They had nothing to do with the big plot against Sir Charles Gilson. It was their job to navigate the ship and to ask no questions. They knew nothing of Frick or the Saladiers. They still looked upon Mrs. Rentley as the authorised representative of the financial group that had been behind Ricardo and Muller.

She talked to Foord earnestly. He was a big stolid Dutchman who had spent most of his life among the Dutch East Indies. The other two had been supplied by him to Muller's requirements.

"Zere is vun boss on ziss pridge," he told her in a rumbling voice when she had finished. "Zat boss he iss I. Ja!"

"Then I can count on you?" she urged.

"Ja. Vat I say, zat I do."

She made to speak again but the uproar broke into such appalling pandemonium that he could not hear her words. In the freakish way in which it had been dropping and lifting for some hours the fog had again cleared magically and, below, on the maindeck, both fore and aft, the scene was indescribable.

Until then, a comparatively small number of the criminals had been engaged in the fighting. There were, perhaps, a hundred and fifty or two hundred of them about the deck when Frick gave the signal to those he had already suborned.

Keeler's men had opposed them immediately.

Frick had under-estimated Keeler's influence or he would have waited longer before striking.

But it had looked easy enough to sweep along the deck and seize control while this number offered small resistance. Then, before the thing spread, he would batten down the hatches and have the remainder where he wanted them.

And, at first, it looked as though the thing would be the *coup de main* he intended. Under the two apache gunmen the mob made a desperate rush that swept the fight forward and almost along to the fo'c'sle.

Then the fog had blotted out everything and the whole thing had verged on fizzling into a farce when the air became clear again. This was when Rushton had sped to the fo'c'sle, leaving Mrs. Rentley in the boat.

But what had gone before was no more than a tuppenny ha'penny melee compared to what came now. Curiously enough, it was not the sound of fighting on deck that brought the criminals swarming up from below like rats out of a cesspit. It was the pitching into the forward hold of the one man early in the fight that told those below decks that something unusual was afoot. And some of Keeler's men guessed what it might be.

Now, watching from the bridge, Mrs. Rentley saw them coming up in their scores. It seemed incredible that any one ship could house such a ghastly collection of creatures as appeared now.

Blear-eyed, dirty, verminous, drunken brutes they were, with little of the human about them. For days, many of them had never appeared on deck. They had been content to wallow and stew below.

But now the lust to kill was upon them. The smell of blood was in their nostrils; the acrid taste of smoke in their mouths.

It seemed impossible that more than a few could possibly know on which side they were fighting. They saw a battle royal proceeding and, with the exception of a small percentage, they dived into the affray at the nearest point.

Frick couldn't have chosen a better moment psychologically. The scum were ripe for anything to break the boredom of the life they had been forced to lead. It is only a marvel that there had not been more killings. Keeler had been right when he warned Muller that they were getting restless.

The whole of the maindeck was a seething mass of struggling men, half-naked, ragged, cursing, sweating beasts who shot and knifed like madmen, caring not where bullet struck or knife went home so long as blood ran.

There wasn't room for every man to stand on the deck. Many were forced out of the melee like pips squeezed out of an orange, some to go plunging down the open hatches or over the side, others to find precarious foothold among the boats and rigging.

Mrs. Rentley saw that the bridge could never be kept clear if they rushed it. A machine-gun at each ladder might do the trick, but nothing less.

Suddenly she spied Rushton. He and Keeler were in the thick of it in the waist. Jonas was isolated like a black island with a dozen or more ruffians trying to reach him. He was grinning broadly as usual and laying about him with fanatic joy.

Then the fog swept in again and the whole picture was blotted out.

The fighting degenerated into a wild scramble without conscious direction. Rushton had not been ready to have matters precipitated. Frick had played a master card in striking so soon. But the fog was the real victor.

A good half of the criminals had no idea why they were fighting. Others had only a vague idea that there was a prize somewhere in the offing but who was to give it or what it would be they hadn't the ghost of a notion.

A few knew well enough that the people who had taken over control of the ship were split into two factions. With Muller and Ricardo gone and Mrs. Rentley in eclipse they were ready enough to throw in their lot with Frick and the Saladiers. Keeler's promises were not backed up by any outward show of power. It was difficult to believe that vast sums of money could be produced by one who skulked in hiding as did Keeler's mysterious principal.

The loyalty of such a mob was a thing that veered with every wind of circumstance. They were ripe for anything and they were anybody's man who would pay most.

Thus it was that matters fell more or less as Frick desired and an incident was to occur that was to appear to consolidate his position beyond danger. This was the disaster that overtook Rushton.

It was very shortly after Mrs. Rentley had seen him fighting in the waist that the thing happened. There were plenty of the ruffians who knew that the desperate looking fellow with the patch over one eye was Keeler's principal. And, knowing this, they made combined and desperate efforts to reach him.

In the wild confusion that reigned it was impossible for any concerted effort to be made.

It was each man for himself and, although Rushton and Keeler had managed to remain close together during the first part of the struggle, they became separated eventually.

Two of the gang who had gone over to Frick had been trying to reach Rushton for some time. Others were making determined attacks upon Keeler and Jonas. They seemed to know that, with these three out of the way, the whole opposition would collapse.

It was when Rushton was in the thick of a mêlée quite alone that their chance came. They were behind Rushton when the fog shut down again but they marked him as a blur upon which they converged.

The barrel of a pistol caught Rushton on the back of the head. It was no love tap, and he went down as if he had been pole-axed. At the same moment, a great surge of the combatants carried Keeler and Jonas with their remaining followers back along the deck, leaving Rushton's body quite isolated.

Yet, even had the fog not come down again, Mrs. Rentley might not have seen what happened to Rushton, for amongst those swaying bodies and tossing heads and arms she had picked out one torso, naked to the waist that held her spellbound with surprise.

He was a giant of a fellow with massive shoulders that were coarse now with rolls of fat but which once had moved under slick supple muscles. His chest, his back and arms were covered with ornate tattoo patterns and it was this display of crude art that brought sudden recognition into Mrs. Rentley's eyes. Without that she would not have pierced beneath the tangled beard that covered half his face and neck.

The present scene vanished to her in more ways than one. It was not only the fog that obliterated it. She was back in the past, ten years before, under the 'Big Top' with the smell of sawdust and the hot stench of animals in her nostrils.

She could see herself, a slim, lithe figure in pink tights beneath an acetyline flare. Opposite her, also in tights, a magnificent specimen of bone and muscle, was Steve Rentley, her husband. In those days the Rentleys were a good turn in the circus world.

She could see Steve throwing small blue glass balls into the air. She could feel again the quiver of her finger as she fired at the spinning globes, six times in as many seconds and each time a globe would be shattered.

But that was only the preliminary of their turn, a spectacular scene to get the attention of the crowd for the famous diving swallow, one of the most daring trapeze turns ever attempted. But it was where she had learned how to shoot with such amazing accuracy.

She could see herself again on that last night as she was pulled up to her trapeze. The faces of the upturned audience were small white patches as she looked down upon them while she sat negligently on the bar wiping her hands.

She could see Steve being pulled up to his trapeze and then came the vivid sensation of swinging as they worked higher and higher to the correct swing for the 'diving swallow.'

And then the moment when, up close to the roof of the 'Big Top' she came down in her last plunge to let go and fly as gracefully as any bird towards the approaching hands that Steve was holding ready to meet her clasp.

But on that night she missed them, not through any error of judgment on her part but because she knew that, at the critical moment, Steve had jerked his hands the veriest trifle to one side.

She went diving towards the ground. A wave of hysteria swept the horrified audience as they saw that plunge to what seemed certain death.

And it would have been death but for a circumstance that could not have been foreseen.

Almost beneath the trapezes but a little to one side, a clown was lending a hand in the erection of a small net to be used in another turn.

At the first gasp of horror from the benches he gazed up, saw the woman diving towards him, made a wild effort to swing the net across beneath her, managed to achieve enough to break her fall partially and then was jerked a dozen feet away as the edge of the net was ripped from his grasp.

But it saved Vesta Rentley's life. Her poor body was a mass of broken bones. For weeks she lay in hospital while the breaks slowly mended.

When she came out Steve was gone. No one but she knew that the thing had been a deliberate attempt on Steve's part to murder her. She heard of him here and there in the circus world. Then news came to her that he had left England with the wife of a juggler.

What course he had travelled during those years she didn't know. But he had wound up as one of the lost six hundred souls in the Ship of the Accursed.

She went down the ladder like a wraith, and with the fearless persistency of a Hazara woman seeking her man on the field of battle, she plunged into that pit after Steve Rentley.

CHAPTER XXI

LIKE wild beasts they lay licking their sores and wounds.

Keeler and his adherents had either been driven below or into the fo'c'sle, which was now barricaded. Keeler and Jonas were there but Rushton had vanished.

The Frick party controlled the ship for the present. But the casualties had been heavy. The deck was littered with groups of wounded, lying as near the rum casks as they could crawl. No one paid the slightest attention to the dead. There was plenty of time to heave them over the side.

No one had eyes for the cloaked figure that slipped among them. Scarcely an eye witnessed the figure vanish over the coaming of the afterhatch and start down the ladder that led into the smoky, foetid bowels of the ship where men lay about in an indescribable condition of blood, drunkenness and dirt.

But the woman who had been bred among the hot animal smells of the circus, who had already become acclimatised to this box of stinking human derelicts, made nothing of such miasmic horror.

She descended the iron rungs until she reached the 'tween decks, where rough cubicles to accommodate a couple of hundred or so of the criminals had been knocked up. Steve Rentley had been about to go down that same ladder when she had last seen him. She intended to find him. And she did.

He was squatting on his hunkers in a small cubicle alone. He was begrimed with dirt and blood but his attention was concentrated on a bottle of rum from which he was drinking greedily.

The woman paused to watch him for a moment. He was unaware of her presence until she stepped into the place and stood before him. Then, as if she were a sudden apparition that had found form in the alcoholic fumes that seethed in his brain, he stared at her owlishly.

"G'way," he muttered, waving the bottle back and forth, "g'way. Don' wan' you here."

She watched him with heavy contempt. Then she brought out her hand and in it was a pistol. She sat down close enough to push the pistol into his ribs.

"Put down that bottle," she snapped. "I'm no vision you'll find. I'm Vesta right enough. You've been guzzling down here since I came aboard or you would have seen me."

He set the bottle between his legs and in his eyes began to grow a look of amazed belief.

"V-Vesta," he stammered, "you—here."

"I'm here right enough, Steve. You thought you were nicely rid of me, didn't you? Ten years it is since you tried to murder me. But no one knows that but you and me, Steve. No one saw you twist your hands so I would miss them. But we knew, didn't we, Steve? We know that you committed something worse than just plain decent murder—the unpardonable sin among circus folk. If I had told the truth you never would have got out of England with your juggler's woman, Steve. Circus folk settle their own affairs of that sort. And now you're here among this scum. Well, well, I suppose you murdered the juggler woman when you tired of her. Is that what happened?"

He was eyeing her with sullen bloodshot eyes. In them was fear of a kind that held him silent. For ten years he had believed her dead and now here she was as mocking, as lithe, as youthful as ever. He could not believe her real.

She laughed, but there was no mirth in the sound.

"All these years our paths have been winding and twisting just in order to meet here in this shipful of scum. Who says there is no such thing as Destiny, Steve? Not I any more. And now that we have met again, my fine murdering fellow, I'm going to hang on to you. Put that bottle down!"

He had started mechanically to lift the bottle to his lips but as she spoke she tore it from his grasp and hurled it out so that it continued on down the hatch to the very bottom of the ship.

And he did not resist. He sat like one in a trance while she talked to him and brought him under her will. Then she rose.

"See that you don't fail me," she warned him.

He could have killed her with a single blow of his great fist. He could have twisted her neck and pitched her after the bottle and none would have exacted an accounting. But he didn't lift a hand. He only nodded and mumbled in obedience to her words and when she had vanished up the ladder, climbing with an agility she had never lost, he rose and began to search for the man she had described.

She reached the deck and made her way to the saloon. She was just in time to find a session in progress.

Frick was sitting at one end of the table with the Saladiers on either side of him. The two van Korsens were together as usual but it was plain that they had now thrown in their lot with Frick. Mrs. Rentley found herself somewhat alone when she coolly took the chair at the other end of the table. She realised that she had suddenly become isolated. Nothing had been said but there was veiled hostility in the eyes of the Saladiers as they watched her and Frick openly avoided even glancing at her. She sat alone as the only active force left of the gang that had been represented by herself, Muller and Ricardo. The two apache gunmen kept guard at the door, they were creatures of the Saladiers.

But there was nothing in her manner or expression to betray her realisation of this situation. She smiled generally at the others and lit a cigarette. Then, under lowered lids, her eyes watched Frick.

"I think we may say that the position is now well in hand," he was saying. "We have gained control of the ship and we shall keep control. The next step is to smash what opposition still exists in the fo'c'sle. Our man, Sir Charles Gilson, is there. It will not take long to smoke them out and then I shall soon attend to him. But there is something else about which I want to speak."

He paused and looked straight at Mrs. Rentley.

"There is one person here whose actions I do not understand," he went on curtly. "I have positive evidence that she—I do not think we need make any mystery about it—has been in communication with the people in the fo'c'sle. Perhaps you will explain, Mrs. Rentley."

"Certainly," she drawled. "We might as well clear the air. I was never strongly in favour of making a deal with you. But I was over-ruled by Muller and Ricardo. I believed that the man who had stolen the plans was still on board the ship. They thought otherwise. If I was right then we didn't need you. We could have got all we wanted out of him. I was afraid, you see, that you would try to double-cross us and now, of course, it is perfectly obvious that you are doing so."

A hissing sound escaped the lips of the countess as she exhaled sharply. The others leant forward to watch Mrs. Rentley more closely. Everyone knew that the showdown had come.

"I prefer to put it that you have been double-crossing us," said Frick coldly. "You have been seen to establish contact with the enemy."

"I acknowledged that. You will probably not believe the truth but I will tell it. I went into the fo'c'sle alone with one object in view—to regain possession of the plans."

"Indeed?" sneered Frick. "And did you do so?"

"I did."

The countess gave another gasp at the crisp answer, but Vesta Rentley was watching Frick. She knew that he was the one she must watch.

"In that case I have been mistaken," he said smoothly. "If you will put the plans on the table we can get to work on them at once."

"I haven't them any longer."

"I thought not. Would you tell us how you managed to part with them?"

"Grant Rushton took them away from me." An incredulous smile went round the table. Frick flushed with sudden anger. He struck the table hard.

"Enough of this fooling," he blazed. "I was glad you came in while we were all here as I had decided to tell you that, since we cannot trust you, we are going to count you out. You will keep away from the deck altogether. If you make no trouble you will be allowed to move between your cabin and this saloon. But that is all. Do you understand?"

Vesta Rentley did not take her eyes off him but, out of the corners she was aware that the two gunmen by the door had moved a little closer.

She weighed the chances of whipping up her gun and shooting Frick. She could do the job she was sure but she realised that the two gunmen would riddle her with bullets before she could gain her feet. Not yet was the moment.

She turned her gaze to the van Korsens. They would not look at her. She looked at the countess whose eyes were maliciously triumphant. There had been no love lost between the two women from the first and the countess had not forgiven the shooting of the Brown Priest. She knew now who had done that.

So Vesta Rentley shrugged and rose.

"Very well," she said quietly. "I'll leave you to your pleasant little party. May I ask what you propose doing with me eventually?"

"If you behave yourself you will be allowed to remain on board," snapped Frick. "You can then make your own arrangements to get ashore when we finish with the scum."

"Very well. I shall leave it at that."

She looked utterly beaten as she turned away and made for the door. The van Korsens looked at each other in surprise to see how meekly she had taken her defeat. They were remembering how she had handled Muller and Ricardo.

But they did not see her face once she had closed the door behind her. They did not see her eyes quicken with anger nor the smile that appeared on her lips. That smile boded no good for Frick.

She went along the corridor slowly. She paused once to look back before she turned into the short gangway leading to her own cabin. Then she stepped briskly to the door and opened it quietly.

On the threshold she paused for a moment to survey the interior. Frick would have been highly interested to view that scene for, sitting on the side of a bunk with a cigarette in one hand and a glass of rum in the other, was a ragged looking fellow with a black patch over one eye.

CHAPTER XXII

RUSHTON greeted her appearance with a twisted grin.

She locked the door behind her and put a finger to her lips. Then she sat down on the bunk beside him.

"Well, so he found you all right."

"I don't know who found me, dear lady, but some ruffian was good enough to drag me out from some hole below and bring me round with a swig of rum strong enough to revive an elephant. Then I was carried along and dumped in here with orders to remain quiet. I suppose I am to thank you for this unexpected hospitality."

"It was on my instructions, yes."

"Well, now that I am your prisoner again what do you propose doing with me? Let me warn you now that I have not the plans. I tossed those into the fo'c'sle just after I left you in the boat."

"The plans can wait. I had you brought here so that Frick's searchers wouldn't find you. Things have happened since you left me in the boat."

Rushton touched the back of his head gingerly.

"I'll say they have," he murmured. "I'd like a few minutes with the blighter who cracked me on the skull."

"You'll get your opportunity if you listen to me."

He cocked a suspicious eye at her.

"What—another deal?"

"Just that."

"You are rather persistent, aren't you. You seem to be spending most of your time offering me terms of one sort or another."

She frowned.

"Be quiet. You do not understand the situation that has developed. Listen to me."

She told him in a low tone how things stood, how his own supporters were barricaded in the fo'c'sle, how Frick's adherents had gained a victory, and how Frick and the Saladiers had coolly welshed on her.

"And so you have figured some way how you think you can use me as a stopgap," he said.

"You will be foolish not to listen to me. Frick holds the whip hand just now. But there is a chance to turn the tables on him. And let me remind you that, once he gets his hands on Sir Charles Gilson, he will have his way with him. He dare not let Sir Charles live now. He will kill him, I tell you, and let it be thought that it was Muller or Ricardo or me who did it. You must see his danger."

"Oh, I see his danger all right," said Rushton quietly. "But you will not be surprised that I do not look to you to succour Sir Charles. If you have double-crossed Frick and the Saladiers I am not going to give you a chance to double-cross me."

Her eyes flashed angrily.

"You speak of double-crossing after what you did to me."

"We were at war and all is fair. I wouldn't blame you for what you did to me but I'm not going to give you a chance, that's all."

"Listen anyway to what I have to say. You think that Keeler and his crowd may have a chance against Frick's gang. They won't. They are too few. Nor will Frick's mob hold their present position if I decree otherwise. It is I who hold the key to the whole situation."

Rushton regarded her sceptically.

"I have a great belief in your capability, dear lady, but I believe now that you are bluffing."

"Then how do you suppose I arranged for you to be found among all that drunken scum and brought here without anyone knowing?"

He gave a soundless whistle.

"I hadn't thought of that. It did take some arranging I'll bet."

"I went down into the hold myself. I tell you that I control forces that are growing every moment. Even now my agents are at work. If you come in with me we can soon settle Frick and the Saladiers. And it is I who still control the bridge and the engine-room."

"And what are your terms?"

"Ten per cent of what Sir Charles may realise on the deal."

"I am not authorised to commit him in such a way."

"Then let me talk to him. The only thing I ask of you is to promise that you will back me up and stick to it. You owe me something for what I have done."

Grant Rushton was silent. Despite the various encounters there had been between him and Vesta Rentley he did not bear her the slightest ill-will. On the contrary, he had considerable respect for her quick wit and daring and now, if she was speaking the truth, admiration for the desperate fight she was making to retrieve her lost position.

If Frick was really in control then the position was bad enough. Had it been only a question of himself he would have trusted to his own wits to find a way out. But there was Sir Charles, an old man and a very important man. And there was Cara Hume. He wondered if he were justified in turning down these proposals without giving Sir Charles a chance to pass on them. He did not think so.

But it will never be known just how far that argument weighed in Grant Rushton's answer. It was something else that decided him. And it came in the form of a low, urgent knocking at the door.

The woman made a cautioning gesture to Rushton and signed for him to move along to the end of the bunk where the open door would partially conceal him unless someone stepped right into the cabin. Then she pulled out her pistol and laid her head against the door.

"What is it?" she asked in a low tone.

"It is I, my dear," came the answer in a woman's voice. "Let me in, I want to speak to you."

Mrs. Rentley shot a quick look at Rushton and turned the key. As she opened the door she drew back, lifting her weapon as she did so. And then, with such deafening suddenness did the explosion come that Rushton was startled into leaping to his feet.

For someone outside the door had fired point-blank at Mrs. Rentley the moment she opened the door and she, he found later, had shot just the fraction of a second sooner.

He thought the murderous attack must have come from the countess whose voice he had recognised but as he flung out from behind the door he saw one of the apache gunmen lying on the floor and had a fleeting glimpse of the countess as she fled round the end of the branch corridor.

Frick had not been content to leave Mrs. Rentley to her own devices. When she had retired he had had one of the gunmen follow her and spy upon her. This fellow had heard voices in her cabin. When he reported the fact, the countess had returned with him to decoy Vesta Rentley to open the door. Then it had been planned to shoot her down in cold blood and eliminate her as a danger once and for all. Frick would have done better to know his woman before taking a step of that sort.

But whatever happened now it meant that Rushton could no longer remain there. Nor could Vesta Rentley. Half a dozen guns would be out after them both within a few moments.

Rushton bent down swiftly and caught hold of the gun that had fallen beside the dead man. Then he felt the woman grasp his fingers.

"We've got to get out of here," she jerked. "Do we go together?"

And Rushton nodded. In common decency then he couldn't have done anything else.

They dashed out of the cabin and into the main corridor. From here they turned to the right so as to reach the companionway that had proved useful to Rushton before.

The fog had cleared again. The atmosphere on the deck seemed sullen and subdued, though one group of ruffians was singing the chorus of a ribald song.

They knew that Frick would be out in pursuit soon if he had not already started. It would mean that he would call upon as many of the criminals as would answer to sweep the ship from stem to stern.

Rushton pulled up when he saw Mrs. Rentley stop suddenly and clutch at a bearded giant. He didn't know it was Steve Rentley. Mrs. Rentley motioned him on.

"Get to the fo'c'sle," she snapped. "Get it open. Leave this to me."

Rushton went on. He passed the open fore hatchway and reached the caboose. He swung round that and brought up against the door of the fo'c'sle. He began to hammer on it with the barrel of his pistol.

"Keeler, come on, quick!"

He heard excited voices inside and could distinguish that of Cara Hume. Then the authoritative tones of Sir Charles Gilson rose above the others.

"Is that you Rushton?"

"Yes—quick."

There was the rattle of timbers and the door swung open. He saw the face of Sir Charles against the gloom; then he caught sight of Keeler, Cara Hume and, like a black fiend behind them, the grinning Jonas.

He slipped inside but when they would have closed and barricaded the door again he stopped them.

"Wait. Listen."

Somewhere aft shooting had broken out. There was no shouting or screaming but a growing murmur that had a sinister menacing sound.

"What is it, Rushton?" Sir Charles insisted.

"I'll explain in a minute, sir. We've got to keep the way open for a bit. How many men have you got here, Keeler?"

"Maybe fifteen."

"Able to fight?"

"Yes."

"Get them ready. We'll be in the thick of it soon. Ah!"

He broke off as a small figure came flying along the deck. He stood aside so that Mrs. Rentley could enter without stopping. She drew up before the astounded Sir Charles.

"Have you told him?" she demanded of Rushton.

"I haven't had time yet."

"What is it?" Sir Charles demanded sharply. "Things have happened, sir. Frick is in control. This woman can swing a large number our way she says. She wants to make a deal."

"If there is to be more fighting there is no time to discuss matters now."

"That is what I say, sir. Would you be prepared to leave it to me to deal with her?"

"Yes, though I don't know why we should."

"There is no time to explain now." He caught Mrs. Rentley by the arm. "Will that satisfy you?" She looked up into his eyes.

"Yes," she told him coolly, "but if you double-cross me again I'll kill you."

There was no uncertainty of light now. From the bridge two searchlights blazed out suddenly, one sweeping forward and one aft. The whole disordered deck of the *Santa Cruz* was thrown into brilliant exposure, the men staggering back half blinded as the dazzling beams stabbed hither and thither.

Mrs. Rentley vanished as swiftly as she had come. Rushton had begged Sir Charles to remain in the fo'c'sle and, calling to Keeler, was racing along the deck.

At that moment, men began to pour out of the forward hatch like so many rats. Rushton feared an ambush, but he found Mrs. Rentley again beside him.

"They're our men," she shouted through the din. "They know what they have to do. I'm going up on the bridge."

He saw her climbing the ladder with the agility of a monkey, then he found himself in the thick of a press of men that was surging aft. From that moment, for the next half hour, he had no coherent idea of what was happening.

It had not taken Frick long to realise that he was in danger. He realised all too late that Mrs. Rentley had not come to that meeting in the saloon without a very strong card up her sleeve. It had been a fatal mistake to give her a chance to play it, but it was no use now wasting time in vain regrets.

The moment the countess rushed in to report the shooting of the apache gunman and the escape of Mrs. Rentley with some ruffian, Frick guessed the truth.

Rushton! She had been in touch with him all along and had been steadily double-crossing him. He didn't know the real depth and twists of the intrigue and counter-intrigue that had been rife on board that hell-ship.

There was some delay while the ruffians were stirred into action once more. It was a delay that was fatal to Frick. In those moments Mrs. Rentley was able to reach Steve Rentley and give him the signal. By the time Frick's mob started down the deck the way was blocked by a solid mass of men and Rushton was coming along with Keeler's gang.

Half an hour later, one of the van Korsens and the second apache gunman were among the other dead and wounded. Frick, the Saladiers and Hugo van Korsen were barricaded in the saloon. The positions had been reversed.

But there was one incident during that fight that was no more seen than one that had taken place beneath the 'Big Top' some ten years before.

Up on the bridge, Vesta Rentley stood watching the struggle that waged back and forth. Beside her was one of the searchlights which illuminated the waist at her feet.

Here, close to the edge of an open hatch two men fought with naked knives. There was little to choose between them. Both were giants, both were coarsened by dissipation, both were fighting with as little regard for orthodox rules as two jungle beasts.

Quietly, Vesta Rentley's hand went up until her fingers closed on the control switch. They rested there for a few moments while she watched the progress of the duel between these two. Then, suddenly, she cut off the light.

For some seconds she held it thus while fresh pandemonium broke beneath her. When she turned it on the glare struck full into the face of one of the two combatants she had been watching.

He stumbled blindly. In the confusion caused by the dazzle his antagonist leaped in and struck home, then lifted his foot and drove it hard against the other's body while he twisted his knife out. There was a moment while the stricken one reeled on the edge of the hatch coaming before pitching into the abyss beneath. As he went, Vesta Rentley nodded her head.

"You didn't deserve that, Steve," she muttered, "but I've got to settle with you yet."

And she was smiling to herself while Steve Rentley, never realising what had saved him, plunged afresh into the fray.

CHAPTER XXIII

A VAST and sultry quiet pervaded the *Santa Cruz.*

The Canaries and Madeira were both left behind. The next dawn to flame up above Africa should reveal the floating drome at her anchorage.

Reaction had set in upon the *Santa Cruz* That portion of the afterguard represented by Frick, the Saladiers and Hugo van Korsen were still imprisoned in the saloon. The old music saloon and the cabins along the starboard side were being used by Sir Charles, Cara Hume and Rushton. Mrs. Rentley had taken up quarters in one of the cabins on the bridge deck. Rushton had only caught an occasional glimpse of her since the night when she had thrown her weight into his side of the scales.

But he had little time to devote to speculation upon her motives. She must be dealt with, he knew, before they reached the drome. At the moment, however, he was concerned with holding the situation in hand as it was and attending upon Sir Charles.

It was the night before they were due to sight the floating drome that Sir Charles sent for him and closed the door.

"Well, that job is done, Rushton," he said tapping the plan upon which he had been at work. "There is the key of the whole thing. It isn't much, no more than a gadget you might say, but it means all the difference in the world. Without this bit of casting the floating drome would be no better than the ex-aircraft-carrier that is lying out there. But I'll show you when it is cast and fixed. It will keep the water inside the drome circle as smooth as a millpond and the drome itself will stand as steady as a lighthouse. Of course the machinery does the trick but this little fellow controls it. And it is this that our friends have been gunning after. But I'm talkative and you're not a mechanic. Yet this is the child of my own brain and I'm proud of it. It means millions, Rushton."

"No wonder others were after it, sir. It has cost a good many lives already."

The hard-bitten old shipowner nodded soberly. "True enough, but we didn't start it. Greed, my boy, greed. It knows no laws. And that reminds me. What are we going to do about our prisoners? I know what I'm going to do about Frick, the traitorous blackguard. To think that he fooled me for so long! I never had the slightest suspicion of him. But I'll be merciless. I'm going to send him up for a few years, and if it wasn't for other considerations I'd push him for murder. But the others—this Saladier gang. I regard them somewhat differently. They are the agents of business rivals and I was prepared for a good fight. We've won, thanks to you."

"I'm afraid you give me too much credit, sir. I've made mistakes."

"We all make mistakes. It is only human to err. But you retrieved yours. What I can't understand is how you managed to bring that she-devil Rentley into line."

Grant Rushton smiled thinly.

"I'm still not quite sure that she didn't bring us into line," he returned. "At any rate, now that we have bottled up Frick and the Saladiers she has gone into a kennel up on the bridge deck. She sees no one and speaks to no one except the bridge crowd, and they have been her men all along."

"She must have her own reasons for what she did. It wasn't for any friendship to us. She will spring a demand before we finish. And I'm not forgetting how she killed poor Green and Follett."

"No, sir, nor am I. I'll deal with her if you leave it to me. She will need watching. She played a master card when she joined in with us to settle the Saladiers. But now she will spring something on us if she gets the chance."

"Then watch her, Rushton, watch her."

"What do you propose about that ex-aircraft-carrier, sir?"

"Do you think they have any suspicion about what has happened here?"

"I don't think so. Nothing goes over the wireless now that I don't censor. Of course we don't know what was sent before."

Sir Charles lit a cigar over which he frowned. It was from the defunct Muller's stock of coarse German stogies, and to a connoisseur like Sir Charles tasted like burnt cabbage. Still, anything was better than no smoke at all.

"It's a wonder Muller wasn't shot long ago—smoking stuff like this," he grumbled. "Look here, Rushton we've got to decide something about that ex-aircraft-carrier. How many men do you think she carries?"

"I shouldn't think more than fifty or sixty, sir. You know that, until you came on the scene with your entirely revolutionary floating drome, she was the only landing spot between the west coast of Africa

146

and the coast of Brazil. Not many cross-ocean planes used her—mostly German and occasionally a Spanish or Italian stunt machine. I suspect, sir, that the Saladiers were employed by the interests who control her. I know that they looked to the people on board her to stand by when they arrived."

"That means we may have trouble when we show up."

"Well, I can swing a good bunch of tough ruffians here, and you have some of your own men aboard the floating drome."

"Between forty and fifty. They've got machine-guns, too."

"Then if we keep things under control on board here we should be able to manage. I propose getting Keeler to furnish me a list of the men who are to receive the reward I promised. I take it you will make arrangements for him to cash in the amount some place in South America?"

"Of course. I shall fulfill whatever promises you made. And that would be the best way to get rid of this outfit when we arrive at the drome— start them off for South America and let them land where they can. We can leave it to your man Keeler to make his own arrangements about paying them."

"Very good, sir. And the Saladiers?"

"If the ex-aircraft-carrier pushes off they go with her. If not—if we have trouble we'll send them on under Keeler's guard to South America."

"That would be the best plan, I think."

"And the Rentley woman? What about her?"

"I'll try and get the strength of her, sir."

Sir Charles nodded and turned back to give his drawing a final checking. Rushton took his dismissal and left him but, as he closed the door, he was by no means certain how to approach Mrs. Rentley. He had a very uneasy feeling that she still held a strong card to play and that she would play it to his discomfiture when he least expected.

He found Cara Hume and took her up to the poop deck. It was the first time for many hours that Rushton had spoken to her alone. But now when he expected to find her willing to talk freely he found her strangely reserved.

There were several things he had planned to say, but in the face of her silence found it impossible. He spoke briefly about the drome and how they expected to sight her the following day.

"I don't know what will happen then," he said somewhat curtly, "but I want you to remain in your cabin as much as possible—that is, if you think you can trust me."

She looked at him and nodded. She opened her lips as if to speak, but Rushton, hurt by her manner, turned and went forward.

It was just after first dawn the next morning when they sighted the drome. And, only a short distance away was a smaller object—the ex-aircraft-carrier. Twin plumes of smoke were drifting from her squat funnels, but the great bulk of the floating drome looked dead.

Sir Charles Gilson and Rushton were on the bridge. Mrs. Rentley was alone in the chart room. They could see her through the glass.

Keeler and Jonas were strutting about the deck, both heavily armed and both very conscious of the position of power they now held.

Cara Hume was still in her cabin. She had obeyed Rushton to the letter. But she was up and already in a dressing-gown when he went down.

"We've sighted the drome," he began.

"I know. I saw it through the porthole. Am I to come up?"

"Yes, Sir Charles advises it," he lied. "Come up on the bridge."

"Very well. I shall be up in a few minutes."

He returned to the bridge at once, for he had a feeling that his job was by no means finished. Mrs. Rentley was still an unknown quantity, and he was uneasy about her.

When he reached the bridge he saw, a little to his surprise, that she had come out of the chart room. She was standing in a wing of the bridge with one of the bridge crew beside her. She had a pair of glasses focussed on the distant drome, but he saw her lower them every few moments and look down into the gang of criminals that was packed on the main deck.

The great floating aerodrome was now plainly visible, and, as one saw it at anchor in mid-ocean, it was possible to realise just what a marvellous steel mammoth had been born of Sir Charles Gilson's brain.

It looked huge beside the ex-aircraft-carrier. The tugs that had brought it on its last stage from Las Palmas were no more than toys lying beside it.

In actual construction the drome was a most massive affair of steel riveted plates forming a huge circular drum fully two thousand feet in outer diameter or more than a mile in outer circumference.

Running the full course of the top was a smooth landing platform two hundred feet wide, that, forming a complete circle as it did, allowed a machine to make a landing against the wind from any quarter. In the same way a plane could take off under any conditions.

From the inner edge of this landing platform the whole centre was an enclosure of sea which, with the vast bulk of the float acting as an endless breakwater, and the special stabilising machinery which Sir Charles Gilson had invented, would be calm water no matter how heavy a tempest might be raging outside. It would form thus an available alighting place for seaplanes in all weather.

The smooth landing surface of the float was some forty feet above the surface of the sea and below the surface there was a further sixty feet of drum, riveted like the rest, in which many thousands of tons of ballast had been dumped.

In the portion above the water, were situated the living quarters of officers and crew, the engine-rooms, special machinery, fuel and other stores, repair shops, petrol and oil tanks for machines in transit and what not, the whole being lighted by means of heavy glass portholes that ran right round the side of the float.

At opposite sides, north and south, were two tall latticed steel beacons carrying the wireless receiving and transmitting aerials. Then, on a small steel mast on the top of these, flew Sir Charles Gilson's house flag. The whole drome was brilliantly flood-lit at night, thus forming a glowing haven for night landing.

It was, in effect, a wonderful creation and, gazing at it for the first time, Grant Rushton could understand why it had roused the desperate greed of unscrupulous forces. Whoever possessed that floating drome and its secret of control held the key of future trans-oceanic air-traffic—and the profits of it.

Something caused him to turn and watch Mrs. Rentley. She had been staring at the great structure and Rushton saw that her face was pale with some suppressed emotion. Was she too realising for the first time just how terrific a prize it was? Would she still try to make some move to retrieve her position?

He could not see how it was possible for her to do so. They were drawing nearer every moment. Now it was plain enough to see men standing at the outer guard rail of the float watching the approach of the *Santa Cruz*.

They knew by wireless messages sent by Rushton that Sir

Charles was coming in this ship. And everything seemed so normal that it looked as though the gang on board the ex-aircraft-carrier had not yet offered any attack. They were probably waiting for definite word from the Saladiers, and deeply puzzled that none had come.

But Rushton was not worrying about them. The ancient carrier was out of the running now. It should be easy enough to take care of her crew. The Saladiers were harmless.

So close were they now to the drome that it looked as if they were running right down upon her.

Rushton touched Sir Charles on the arm.

"About time to signal the engine-room, sir."

"I was thinking that. You give the order, Rushton. Will you speak first to—her?" And he indicated Mrs. Rentley.

Rushton glanced at the man at the wheel. He was a short stubby fellow who stood like a rock hanging on to the spokes with muscular hairy hands. He was gazing straight ahead and another of the bridge crowd was standing over by the wing near Mrs. Rentley.

There was something about the positions they occupied that seemed to strike Rushton for the first time. It was as if they had kept together at that end deliberately. And at this moment the third member of the bridge crowd came out of the chart room. It struck Rushton forcibly that these three were probably still Mrs. Rentley's men.

He was standing uncertainly when someone came up the bridge ladder. It was Cara Hume. He motioned her to stand by Sir Charles and then he moved forward to speak to Mrs. Rentley.

But before he had taken three steps she turned, and then Rushton stopped. She was covering him with an automatic pistol.

"Stand where you are," she ordered curtly. "I shall signal the engine-room at the proper time."

Rushton measured the space between them. He knew she wasn't bluffing. She had had some card up her sleeve as he had half suspected, and now she was going to play it. But what was it? What could she do?

He could see over the rail to where the ex-aircraft-carrier lay. The drome was behind him. But a mocking smile in the woman's eyes told him the truth. Sir Charles had seen it too, for Rushton heard him swear violently.

At that, Rushton leaned forward. Mrs. Rentley fired point-blank.

It would have been a miracle had she missed at that range, a miracle unless something intervened. But something did intervene. On the same moment there was another explosion, the two sounding as one. Rushton was untouched but Mrs. Rentley whirled round sharply as a bullet crashed into her shoulder. Rushton didn't know then it was Cara Hume who had fired that bullet.

Mrs. Rentley was clinging to the rail trying to get her gun up again. Down beneath them a giant of a fellow was rushing for the bridge ladder. It was Steve Rentley.

Rushton paused. There was a drama rushing to its crisis before his eyes in which he had no part. The woman had swung away from the rail. Steve Rentley was almost at the top of the ladder when he looked up to find her at the top. For a long moment, while the Ship of the Accursed rushed to her doom they looked at each other. Then, at something he saw in her eyes, Steve Rentley drew back. His hands gripped the sides of the iron ladder. Rushton was amazed at the sudden terror that showed in his eyes. Just a fleeting film-glance it all was, then the woman fired.

Steve Rentley dropped with a bullet through his brain. Rushton leaped for Mrs. Rentley. She was turning and he knew that she was seeking Cara. He reached her and tore the pistol from her hand. She shrank with a gasp of pain as his fingers closed on her shoulder. Rushton eased his grip and found himself looking straight down into her eyes.

"Let me go," she raved at him, "let me go. You'll all come with me in a moment. But I've settled my score with Steve Rentley."

Rushton didn't know what she was talking about. He knew nothing of Steve Rentley or the past between him and this strange woman.

She slid out of his grasp and looked at him again.

"It might have been so different," she told him in a voice that seemed quiet yet clear in all the tumult. "So different—Grant. If I'd known what I know now. But—never mind."

She swayed, and he reached out to catch her. But she pushed him away.

"Leave me alone. Everything is too late now. Tell Sir Charles I'm sorry about those two men of his. I regret nothing else."

Suddenly she sprang forward and, before Rushton knew what she intended, had caught his head and drawn it down. She kissed him on the lips, then she sprang back and he started forward again as he saw her gain the rail. But he was too late. She laughed at him strangely just before she vanished over the side.

A great cry below brought Rushton back to the urgency of the situation. The men were milling, cursing and bellowing hoarsely. The sight was appalling.

Straight in upon the flank of the ex-aircraft-carrier they were driving at full speed. The great bulk of the floating drome was no more than a biscuit-toss away. They were almost past it.

The men at the rail were gazing at them in amazement. The crew of the carrier were staring at them in horror. Nothing that Rushton or anyone else could do would avail now.

Rushton leapt past the man at the wheel and caught Sir Charles.

"Jump, sir, jump," he yelled at him. Sir Charles was rushing towards the rail. Rushton followed him, dragging Cara Hume.

Down below the curses and shouts had died to a horrified silence that broke swiftly like the concerted howl of a pack of wolves. The man at the wheel was letting go the spokes. Sir Charles was over the side. Rushton watched him strike the water. He picked up Cara Hume and tossed her after him.

He saw several others tumble over the rail. Rushton made one last desperate effort to get the wheel over. He saw that it was useless. All the time he was shouting to the mob below to jump.

He thought of Frick and the Saladiers trapped in the saloon and after cabins. Now he knew why Mrs. Rentley had delayed playing her last card until it must have a maximum effect. She was taking ghastly revenge upon those who had double-crossed her.

He dared not delay longer. He was terribly anxious about Cara Hume, but he knew that Sir Charles could swim like a porpoise and trusted to him to give her a hand until he could reach them.

Just before it seemed the collision must come, he raced for the side and went over. He was under water when the air was filled with a deafening pandemonium of splitting steel and timbers, of human cries and curses.

But they were still ringing about him when he broke surface again and saw Sir Charles and Cara Hume.

Boats had been put out from the floating drome with amazing speed. The two little tugs that had towed the wonder-craft from Las Palmas were throwing off warps so as to take a hand in the work. The water was peppered with bobbing heads.

Rushton reached his friends and got on one side of Cara Hume. A boat came up and they were hauled in. Sir Charles looked very white and only half conscious.

Now Rushton could see how the *Santa Cruz* had driven her nose into the flank of the ex-aircraft-carrier like a spearhead, plugging the hole she had made.

For some minutes she hung there, then, to the accompaniment of a sickening grinding sound she sucked clear. A terrible sight followed. The nose of the *Santa Cruz* went down, and up into the air went her stern. For what seemed an interminable time she remained poised thus. Then, suddenly, like the stricken thing she was, she took the plunge. The carrier, freed from the grip of the other rolled over violently, over and over until her top hamper came clattering down upon the sea. Then she followed the other.

It will never be known exactly how many persons were lost in that final reckoning of criminals. Certainly more than half of the company of the Ship of the Accursed went down, and only a score or so were picked up from the carrier.

Frick, the Saladiers and, of course, the van Korsens were never seen. Nor did Rushton catch sight of Mrs. Rentley again. She had played for defeat as coolly as she had ever hazarded for victory. Renunciation? Perhaps.

The survivors were taken care of on board the float. As each dripping man was hauled over the side he was quickly disarmed and hustled into one of the many store-rooms below.

Three days later one of the Gilson Line tramps arrived from Las Palmas in response to a wireless message. The survivors of the Ship of the Accursed were put on board. They would be turned loose at a deserted part of the coast of South America. It was part of the pact that Sir Charles and Rushton had made with Keeler and Jonas, both of whom had been among the first to go over the side of the *Santa Cruz*. They were now in undisputed control of the chastened criminals whose boredom had been smashed in a way they hadn't expected. And Keeler took with him a draft on a certain South American bank that discharged in full the obligations to which Rushton had committed Sir Charles. Jonas stuck close to Keeler. It was a document that represented more money than either had ever dreamed of. And Jonas knew Keeler.

Later, in the course of her cruise the *Corsair* appeared over the horizon. Her passengers who must be given every possible entertainment on such a luxury cruise were to be permitted a privileged view of the great mystery float about which they had only heard vague rumours.

They saw a marvel of peaceful industry and were duly grateful for the flattering privilege of a pre-view. They saw or heard nothing that revealed the very different activity that had prevailed on the same spot a few days before.

Which, perhaps, is just as well.

And then, too, their interest in the float was quickly submerged in another event of a more romantic sort. This was the mysterious reappearance on board the *Corsair* of Grant Rushton and Cara Hume. Only they weren't distinguished now by a difference of names. They were, curiously enough, Mr. and Mrs. Grant Rushton.

THE END.
[57000 words]

www.ingramcontent.com/pod-product-compliance
Lightning Source LLC
Chambersburg PA
CBHW050819180626
46814CB00004B/1373